Dead at the starting gate ...

Captain Pelham stood in front of the desk looking at Bradley.

"Sorry, but I'll have to keep you waiting a moment, Captain. Sit down." Inspector Luke Bradley was thumbing through a sheaf of papers.

Pelham sat down. The nerve at the corner of his mouth would not stay still. He would have been astonished if he could have seen the paper which Bradley was studying with such evident concentration. It was a notice of the annual precinct Christmas party for the benefit of the families of sick policemen.

The captain was getting the "silent treatment." As the minutes passed, he kept crossing and uncrossing his legs and tugging at the end of his mustache. Finally Bradley folded his papers neatly and put them to one side. He gave Pelham a level look.

"All right, Captain, let's get down to brass tacks. Why did you murder your wife?"

Before Bradley could lift a hand, Pelham had lunged across the intervening space and was at his throat.

From the files of
Inspector Luke Bradley

24th Horse
HUGH PENTECOST

The "Inspector Luke Bradley" Series

Cancelled in Red

The 24th Horse

I'll Sing At Your Funeral

The Brass Chill

Rich Harvey
Editor & Designer

"Luke Bradley" photo by
Dmitriy Cherevko

ISBN-13: 978-1530085217
Retail paperback: $14.95

Printed and bound in the United States.
10 9 8 7 6 5 4 3 2 1

Published by Bold Venture Press
www.boldventurepress.com

Edition notes

The 24th Horse by Hugh Pentecost (pen name for Judson P. Philips) was published in 1940 as a paperback and hardcover book.

Inspector Luke Bradley and his shadow, Sergeant Rube Snyder, were secondary characters in Pentecost's debut novel, *Cancelled in Red.* Now they move to center stage as the third-person narrative switches from Bradley's investigation to scenes of the various suspects.

The Saturday Review of Literature said of *The 24th Horse*: "Blackmail in the horsey sets basis of tale with galloping action, glamorous background, some acrid humor and 24-point solution.

An abridged version of *The 24th Horse* appeared in *The American Magazine*, October 1940 (The Crowell-Collier Publishing Company). Illustrations by Earl Cordrey accompanied the story.

The Popular Library paperback (1940) was the source for this edition's text.

1

In one of the sloping entryways to the north side of the arena at Madison Square Garden stood a young man in a dinner jacket, a black felt hat pulled down over his eyes. He had just thrown away a partially smoked cigarette, and immediately he placed a fresh one between his lips. He never got to light it.

There was a roar of applause from the crowd that jammed every nook and cranny of the Garden. This was the fanciest turnout of the year, all top hats, furs, and jewels. Not like the fight customers, not like the bike-races lunatics, not like the hockey fans. This was the inimitable gathering that appears every November for the last night of the National Horse Show.

Down in the tanbark ring the Open Jumping Championship was under way. One by one, riders took their horses around the difficult, crisscross course rail fence and brick wall, triple bar and chicken coop, in-and-out and hedge, guarded by water beyond. One by one the greatest jumpers in the world, from twenty-thousand-dollar thoroughbreds to cold-blooded army mounts bought for a song, tested their mettle against the championship layout.

"Miss Patricia Prayne, Number 71, riding Tangerine," droned

the announcer by the in Gate.

It was then that the young man forgot his cigarette. His blue eyes fastened on the girl bringing a tall chestnut gelding, with the sloping shoulders and high withers of a jumper, through the In Gate.

She was a brown, wiry kind of a girl in a tweed habit, her blonde hair tucked up under a hunting derby. Perched on the chestnut's back, she looked small and tense: but her gloved hands rested lightly on either side of the horse's sleek neck.

Tangerine was quiet. Unlike the last horse, who had been wild-eyed and fretting, he seemed almost bored by the task that lay ahead of him. The girl walked him toward the first jump, let him look at it, and then wheeled back to the starting point.

The young man had jammed his hands into his pockets. His eyes never left the girl as Tangerine broke into an easy lope and the ride was on. The gelding sailed over the five-barred gate without effort. There was confidence in his flowing style. Pat Prayne's hands kept only the slightest contact with his mouth. She did not need to pull her horse down, to fight him for a steady pace. Tangerine knew his job.

Around he went, over brick wall and triple bar. As he approached the tricky in-and-out, the crowd held its breath. Up … down … quick gathering together and up again! Tangerine flicked up his heels and whisked his tail. He was having a good time. Across the diagonal he came, toward the water jump at which a dozen competitors had already refused. His ears pricked forward, but he didn't hesitate. He cleared it by a good three feet.

Sound swelled in the throats of the crowd, not quite a cheer yet. Two more to go … brush and then the chicken coop. The slightest nick and the coop would topple.

Now the brush was behind the chestnut. His pace increased as he rushed at the red-painted obstacle. Up … up! Then a flick of polished hind hoofs and he was clear.

The rafters shook. It was a faultless performance, the first of the evening.

The young man in the entryway took a handkerchief from his hip pocket and mopped at his face. When he turned away, he was confronted by a young couple, also in evening clothes. "Why, Johnny Curtin! You know my wife, Johnny?"

"Hello," said Johnny Curtin. His voice was husky from strain.

"Say," the man said, "that Prayne girl can certainly ride."

"She's okay," said Johnny.

"Isn't she Gloria Prayne's sister?" the woman asked.

"Yes."

The man grinned at Johnny. "You used to go for her, didn't you, Johnny, before you started running around with Gloria?"

A muscle rippled along the line of Johnny Curtin's jaw. "Listen," he said, "why don't you for Christ's sake mind your own business?" He pushed past them into the passage beyond.

"Well, what on earth!" the woman exclaimed.

Her husband laughed. "Good ol' Johnny. Tight as a tick!"

***

Johnny Curtin paused by the stairs leading to the main floor. After a minute he changed his mind, walked around the passageway, and went through the door of the Horse Show Association Room. A couple of men stood at one end of the bar, which stretched along the far wall. Johnny headed for the other end.

"Scotch and soda," he said. He rested his hands, fists still tight, on the mahogany top until the bartender brought his drink. His fingers had just closed over the glass when someone came up beside him.

"Hello, Mr. Severied," said the bartender. "What will it be?"

"Scotch," said a pleasant, drawling voice.

Johnny Curtin's glass stopped halfway to his lips. He held it there for an instant, then drained almost half of it before he put it down. He glanced at the man beside him.

"Hello, Guy," he said.

"Nice ride of Pat's," said Guy Severied. He was tall and broad-shouldered, with blond hair which curled. He wore tails and a topper. His expression was blandly social. Any reporter could have rattled off information about him at a moment's notice. Forty years old … one of the three largest private fortunes in America … nine goals at polo … a yachtsman … and still unmarried, despite major campaigns by the mothers of ten seasons of debutantes.

"No news, I suppose," said Johnny.

Guy Severied's face clouded. "Not a whisper. Johnny, it beats me. I've been every place in town where Gloria would be likely to go. No one has seen hide nor hair of her since … since Wednesday night."

"That," said Johnny, "was the night I took her to, El Morocco."

Severied's lips moved in a faint smile. "Check."

"It's a hell of a note," Johnny said. "Pat's so worried. I was afraid she might muff that ride."

"That isn't all Pat's worried about, Johnny," Severied said.

"It's partly my fault … about Gloria, I mean," Johnny said. "We had a kind of a row and … she left me flat."

"That's standard technique of hers," said Severied. "But three days is a long time to stay way in a pet."

"*You* haven't had a brawl with her, have you, Guy?"

"No-o," said Severied.

Johnny looked up at him. "You know, Guy, I've been expecting you to put the slug on me."

"Why?" asked Severied.

"Damn it, let's not pretend, Guy. You're as good as engaged to Gloria. Then I barge in and give her a rush. Well, if I'd been you …" He stopped.

Severied knocked the ash from his cigarette. "If I did put the slug on you, Johnny, it wouldn't be for that."

"I know," Johnny said bitterly. "If it wasn't too lousy a way out, I'd jump in the creek!"

Severied hesitated, as if he wanted to be certain of choosing just the right words. "Gloria's an amazing' creature," he said finally. "No one's blaming you for having gone overboard. She's turned cooler heads than yours, Johnny. But Pat is quite something, too."

Johnny groaned. "Don't I know it!"

"Do you also know that she's what they call a one-man woman, Johnny? She loves you … and I don t think you could do anything to change that." Severied's tone was dry. "If I were Pat, I would send you packing. But she's not that kind."

"Guy!" Johnny looked up. "You think there's still a chance she might … might …"

"There's no doubt of it. What she sees in you, Johnny, I don't know, but…"

"Gangway!" said Johnny Curtin.

"Mr. Curtin!" the bartender called after him. "Your drink!"

"It's all right," said Guy Severied. He smiled sourly at himself in the glass behind the bar. "The drinks are on me."

***

During the week of the National the Garden basement takes on all the color and trappings of the world of horse. Rows upon rows of box stalls, knee-deep in straw, house the most expensive horseflesh money and breeding can produce. Spotted along these rows are improvised tack rooms, their walls and ceilings formed by bright blankets. Here all the equipment of a stable has its place in a neat array. Blue, red, yellow and white ribbons, records of victories past and present, decorate the walls. Here hang saddles, bridles, and harnesses, soaped until they gleam like polished metal.

From morning till night the place swarms with people — shirt sleeved grooms, riders in boots or jodhpurs, ladies in tailored habits, uniformed officers of the army teams, harried officials and judges, spectators in tails and ermine, secretaries from Wall Street who have "the bug." These latter pause to stare at the horses and to pet an assortment of dogs, cats, goats, and other mascots.

Into this maelstrom moved Johnny Curtin, more like a halfback making an open field run than an ordinary man in a hurry. He saw his objective — the Prayne Stables. He saw Pat. There was a crowd around her, shaking her hand, slapping her shoulders. Suddenly she broke away and started toward the dressing room. Johnny Curtin blocked her path, and she bumped into him with some violence.

"I'm terribly sorry!" Pat said. Then she saw who it was "Johnny!" Eagerness swept over her Face. "Johnny, you've found Gloria?"

"No," he said, watching the light leave her eyes. "To hell with Gloria. She can take care of herself. I'm the one who needs a guardian, Pat! I've been out of my mind. When I saw you out there on Tangerine, I ..."

She cut him off, a brown hand on his sleeve. "I can't talk now, Johnny. We'd be interrupted. I ... I've got to powder my nose, because I'm getting to look like a horse. And there are going to be pictures, and — "

"I've got to talk to you, Pat, now ... tonight."

"Johnny, please! There isn't any use. I understand."

"You do not understand!"

Pat hesitated. "Come for dinner tomorrow. Gloria may be

back by then."

"I've got to talk to you *tonight!"* Johnny insisted.

"But, Johnny! Oh, darn it, I suppose if you must you must." Color had risen in her cheeks. "George and Peter are trucking the horses uptown to the school tonight, so I'll be driving home in the car alone. If you want to meet me outside the exhibitors' entrance about one o'clock ..."

"I'll be there," Johnny said.

***

In the Association Room, Guy Severied was just turning away from the bar when a man came through the door and hailed him. He was tall and slender, with a lined face, brooding eyes, and a clipped black mustache over a firm mouth.

"Thought you'd be up here, Guy," he said. "I need a drink. Can you go for another?"

"Why not?" said Severied. He leaned his elbows on the bar again. "Pat certainly came through for you, George."

"What'll it be, Captain Pelham?" the bartender asked.

"Brandy and soda."

"The same for me," said Severied.

Pelham looked down at his polished riding boots. "This has been one hell of a night. I was nervous about Pat. She's got her mind on Gloria ... like all of us. I was afraid she'd muff it, and with Martinson of the Canadian Army Team ready to lay seven thousand bucks on the line if Tangerine came through. It meant a lot to us."

"Pat isn't the kind to let anyone down, no matter how tough the pressure is," Severied said.

"She's aces," said Pelham. "Here's looking at you." He drank and then set his glass down on the bar. "What *about* Gloria, Guy?"

Severied shrugged. "Playing games of some sort. When she

gets ready to put in an appearance, she will."

"I don't like it," said Pelham sharply.

"Maybe you could suggest something to do about it."

Pelham turned to look squarely at his friend. "Look here, Guy, I've had the feeling for some time that you weren't happy about things. You don't have to go through with marrying Gloria if it's gone sour. We're not living in the Middle Ages any longer, you know."

"Aren't we?" Severied's tone was bitter.

"Guy, if there's some way I could help you …"

"Forget it. Gloria and I are going to marry and spend our lives having fun. You know … night clubs, yachts, bridge parties. Jesus!"

"Guy!"

"Sorry. Doesn't every prospective bridegroom get stage fright at some point? That's my trouble. I think I shall have me a nice private binge tonight."

Pelham regarded him anxiously. "Guy, you know there isn't a damn thing in the world I wouldn't do for you. If there's any way I can help, let me do it. God knows, I can never repay you for the way you've stood by me in the past."

"There's nothing you can do," said Severied, looking fixedly at the whisky in his glass. "Not a cockeyed thing, George."

"So help me," said Pelham, "I'd like to tan Gloria's behind for treating you this way."

Severied laughed. "Reserve me a ringside seat, will you?"

***

Outside the exhibitors' entrance the Praynes' yellow convertible was parked. Johnny Curtin, the collar of his overcoat turned up, paced the sidewalk. It was already after one.

Then Pat appeared, loaded down with a couple of coats, a large silver trophy, a suitcase. Johnny took them from her.

"I thought you were never coming," he said.

"Maybe I'm not here yet, Johnny," she said. "Be an angel. Put these things in the rumble. Here are the keys. I've still got to see two or three people, phone Linda about Gloria, and dish out a couple of tips. I swear I won't be long, Johnny."

"It's your funeral," he said. "When I start talking, you've got to listen till I'm through. It may take all night."

She slipped her hand into his for an instant. "I don't think I'm going to mind." Then she turned back into the building.

Johnny lugged the stuff she had given him over to the curb and unlocked the rumble seat. He stood poised on the rear fender for perhaps thirty seconds. Then he slammed the rumble shut and began piling Pat's stuff into the front of the car, rapidly. When he had finished, he crossed the pavement toward a uniformed policeman.

"Do you know Miss Prayne by sight?" he asked.

"The one that was just talking to you? Sure."

"Look. Tell her I couldn't wait," Johnny said. "When she comes out, tell her I just couldn't wait any longer."

"You taking the car?" the policeman asked.

"Yes." Johnny fumbled in his pocket and took out a bill. "Give her this and tell her she'll have to take a taxi home."

"Maybe she won't like being stood up," the policeman said.

"Maybe she won't," Johnny said. He went to the far side of the car, jumped in, and drove off toward Ninth Avenue.

2

INSPECTOR Luke Bradley of the Homicide Division thrashed restlessly on his bed and at last opened his eyes. Someone was pounding at the door of his apartment. Bradley reached up, turned on the light, and glanced at his wrist watch. Quarter past two!

He felt for his slippers, stood up, and pulled on a blue dressing gown. The pounding continued. Bradley was unhurried. He ran his fingers through his close-cropped red hair, flattened down the collar of the dressing gown, and then ambled over toward the door.

"Hold it!" he said plaintively. "You'll have the house down!" He unfastened the safety chain and swung back the door.

Confronting the inspector was an old gentleman who had been hammering on the door with a bone-handled umbrella. Between the brim of an old-fashioned high-crowned brown derby and the astrakhan collar of a long black overcoat that hung almost to his shoe tops little was visible. From the left-hand pocket of the coat a black metal ear trumpet protruded. He regarded Bradley suspiciously.

"Humph! Carousing," he said. The remark was addressed to

the young man behind him — a young man with a white, drawn face. "Get rid of her!" he added to Bradley.

"Sorry to disappoint you, Mr. Julius," said Bradley. His mild gray eyes were amused. He looked at Mr. Julius' companion.

"This young fool's name is Curtin—Johnny Curtin," said Mr. Julius. "Forget him till I've asked you a question."

"Better come in and ask it," said Bradley. He pressed a switch by the door.

The large room had been remodeled from the kitchen of an old private dwelling. A wide brick fireplace with Dutch ovens took up one side. Burnished copper pots hung from a rack over the mantel, their purpose obviously decorative. There was a couch in front of the fireplace, and one overstuffed armchair. A solid square table beside the couch held a lamp, a blue china bowl filled with pipes, a copper tobacco jar. The inspector's bed, between deep windows, was built into the wall like a ship's bunk. The woodwork and the casement bookcases had been white, but were now mellowed by smoke and age. At the far end was a door, its top half of glass, opening to a small garden.

Bradley waved his visitors toward the couch. There were still embers on the hearth, and he laid some kindling and a couple of apple logs on top of the coals. He worked at them with ancient leather hand bellows until the kindling burst into flame.

Mr. Julius had put his hat, umbrella, and ear trumpet on the table. He removed his overcoat, unwrapped a gray knitted muffler from his neck, retrieved the ear trumpet, and pre-empted the center of the couch. Johnny Curtin waited by the fire, staring at Bradley. As Bradley rose from the hearth, their eyes met.

The inspector's look was friendly, yet it was disconcertingly keen.

"Well?" said Bradley to the old man.

"What's that?" The ear trumpet jutted in Bradley's direction.

Bradley smiled at Johnny. It was a pleasant smile. Despite the deep furrows in his forehead he could not have been more than thirty five. "Experience has taught me," he said, "that you cannot force our friend here to come to the point."

"Of course I can come to the point," snapped Mr. Julius. He seemed to have heard quite well without the ear trumpet. "Came here to ask you a question — technical question. Don't want you hemming and hawing. Answer it straight out."

"I'll do my best," said Bradley. He selected a pipe from the blue bowl and began loading it from the copper jar.

"Point is this," said Mr. Julius. "In the case of a homicide how do you high muckymucks get assigned to the case?"

Bradley grinned. "By the commissioner."

"Suppose a crime is committed in the Bronx? Could you want the body discovered?"

"I could," said Bradley, "if the commissioner thought I was the man for the job. Naturally, the police in the district where the crime takes place would have charge at first."

"Great Scott!" bellowed Mr. Julius. "I ask for a straight answer and what do I get? Does it make any difference in what part of the city the body is found? Could you still be assigned to the case?"

"Yes, if the commissioner — "

"Stop it!" Mr. Julius turned to Johnny. "Told you he'd quibble. Can't come straight out with anything. This is simple, Bradley. We've got a homicide for you. Want you to handle it. Friends of mine involved. Where do you want the body discovered?"

Bradley had struck a kitchen match to light his pipe. Flame burned down the stick until it scorched his fingers. He dropped it with a muttered exclamation.

"Let me get this straight," he said slowly. "You have a homicide for me? Where do I want the body discovered? You can arrange that?"

"Would I ask if I couldn't?"

Bradley struck another match, and this time he got his pipe going. His gray eyes flicked to Johnny. Nothing in that young man's expression suggested a joke.

"Suppose," said the inspector, "we start over. Has this homicide already been committed?"

"Naturally. And don't ask questions! Answer mine!"

"And you propose to move the body so that it will come under my jurisdiction?" Bradley asked.

"If necessary," said Mr. Julius.

"You know it's a crime to move a body until it's been examined by the proper authorities?"

"What do you think a man learns in seventy years? Wouldn't touch a body with a ten-foot pole. But I never heard of any law against moving the *place* where a body is found."

"Moving the place!" Bradley looked at Mr. Julius in awe.

"That's what I said!"

Bradley drew a deep breath. "Would you mind telling me where the body of the victim in your homicide is now?" he asked.

"Of course I don't mind," said Mr. Julius. "It's in the rumble seat of an automobile."

"And where is the car?"

"That," said Mr. Julius with exasperation, "is what we came to find out."

"Mercy!" said Bradley. "You came to ask me where the car is?"

"No, you fool! We came to ask you where it should be if you are to handle the case. The body is in the rumble seat … just where young Johnny there found it."

"And where is the car now?" repeated Bradley. He spaced his words as if he were speaking to a small child.

"The car," said Johnny in a low voice, "is outside your front door. Mr. Julius and I drove here in it."

***

About three quarters of an hour before the arrival of Johnny and Mr. Julius at Bradley's apartment, a taxicab drew up in front of a building on Ninety-First Street, just east of the park. It had once been a storage warehouse, but now the second and third floors had been transformed into apartments with an entrance on Madison Avenue. On the Ninety-first Street side was a wide-arched doorway into which was backed a horse van. To the right of the door a black and gold sign announced that this was the Crop and Spur Riding School run by Captain George Pelham and Miss Patricia Prayne.

Pat Prayne got out of the taxi and handed the driver a bill.

"Keep the change. It's not my money," she said dryly.

She walked past the truck into the Crop and Spur. Powerful lights hanging from the ceiling reflected against whitewashed walls. Across the empty tanbark ring, by the ramp to the air-conditioned stables in the basement, were three men: the truck driver; Peter Shea, the school's head groom; and Captain George Pelham.

Pelham caught sight of Pat and came toward her. "You want to get the car in, Pat? He's taking the truck away now."

Pat laughed, but she wasn't amused. "I don't want to get the car in, George, because I haven't got it. I've been given the finest standing-up of a lifetime."

Pelham's shrewd eyes saw that despite the laughter she was very close to tears. "What's up?" he asked.

"Johnny!" Pat said. "It's really very funny, George. He came tearing down to see me after the Championship … said he had to talk to me now, tonight. Tomorrow wouldn't do. I … I rather got the idea that he'd … well, changed his mind about things. I suggested he wait for me after the show and ride home with me. I carried a lot of junk out to the car and gave it to him to put in the rumble while I said good-by to Mike and some of the others. When I came back, Johnny *and* the car were gone."

"The young pup!" Pelham said angrily.

"But he was very thoughtful, George! Johnny's always the gentleman, you know. He left a dollar with a cop so I'd have taxi fare to get home."

"I'll be damned! What do you suppose was eating him?"

"He told the cop," Pat said, "that he couldn't wait any longer."

"By God," said Pelham, "when I get hold of him I'll — "

"Hush, George. You can't hold Johnny responsible for his actions. He's in love." The smile she gave Pelham was a trifle wistful. "I wish he'd make up his mind with whom."

"Forget him," said Pelham. He slipped an arm around her shoulders. "I haven't had a real chance to tell you how proud I am of you, kitten. You gave Tangerine the best kind of a ride."

"Thanks, George. I … I'm almost sorry Martinson bought him. He's a grand horse."

"Hey, you're in the business now, young'un," Pelham said. "You can't afford to be sentimental. Seven thousand bucks is going to keep away a lot of wolves."

"I know it … darn it," Pat said.

"Speaking of wolves," said Pelham, "your father and Aunt Celia have some kind of supper for us upstairs. Linda's there, too. I promised to take her home afterward."

Pat sighed. "Oh, boy, I could hit the hay for about a month! It … it takes it out of you, George, riding in competition like that."

"You were tops," Pelham said. "Come on. We can slide up the back way."

The Praynes' living room was crowded with furniture

that had plainly come from a more prosperous period in their lives—the sort of pieces which would be given up only in the last extremity.

Douglas Prayne sat in an armchair by a coal grate. He was in his late fifties, his hair graying. He wore tweeds with an air that suggested his country squire, somehow out of place in a New York apartment. He rose as Pat and Pelham came into the room.

"Congratulations, darling!"

Pat stared at him. "You weren't there, Father!"

"Of course I was there. You were magnificent."

"In those clothes!" Pat wailed.

Douglas Prayne looked down at the worn tweed affectionately. "No-o. But I got out of the boiled shirt as soon as I got home.

"You're a beast, Father. I never get a chance to see you dressed up, and you look so darned handsome when you are."

"Well, in any event, I was there. Linda Marsh very sweetly shared her box with Celia and me. They're out in the kitchen now, whipping up a lobster Newburg. Drink, George?"

"Thanks, I'll help myself." Pelham went to a sideboard and poured himself a whisky. "Well, here's to a big year for the Crop and Spur. That ride of Pat's will help."

"I was proud of you," Douglas Prayne said. Then he frowned. "I rather expected Gloria. But I suppose she was somewhere about with friends."

"Of course," said Pat hastily. "I'll see if I can help in the kitchen."

Miss Celia Devon, Pat's aunt, stood by an electric chafing dish in the kitchen, stirring the Newburg. She wore an apron over a black lace dinner dress. Celia Devon had been a beautiful girl, and she was now a handsome older woman. Though she kept house and did the cooking for the Prayne ménage, she always managed to convey the impression that it was "the maid's night out."

"I was beginning to wonder if you were coming home!" she said. "We were about to start without you."

"We were doing nothing of the sort," said Linda Marsh. She was piling bread and butter sandwiches on an oval plate. "After your performance tonight, angel, we'd have waited till doomsday! Pat, I'd give my eyeteeth to ride like that!" Linda Marsh had coal-black hair and a milky skin. Her mouth was smooth and scarlet. She was often referred to as one of the best-dressed women in New York — which wasn't surprising since clothes were her business. Her dress shop on Fifth Avenue did well by both society and Hollywood.

"You'd better come take some lessons," Pat said. "We need the money, darling."

"I wish I had the time."

"I should have thought," said Celia Devon, "that Gloria might have had the decency to stop by the box this evening to speak to her father! We haven't so much as heard her voice for three days. I've been asking Linda what she does with herself, but she doesn't seem to know."

Linda and Pat exchanged a quick glance. "I'm always in bed when she gets in in the evening," Linda said, "and gone to business before she gets up in the morning. I've got her trained."

"In my opinion," said Celia Devon, "it's an imposition for her to spend days at a time with you when she has a perfectly good home of her own."

"But I love having her," Linda said. She busied herself with the sandwiches.

Miss Devon disconnected the chafing dish and lifted, it onto a tray.

"Bring the sandwiches, Linda," she said. "You might take the coffee, Pat."

"Of course, Aunt Celia." The moment the older woman, disappeared, Pat spoke to Linda. "No news?"

"Sorry, darling. Not a word."

"You're sweet to pretend to Father and Aunt Celia' that she's with you," Pat said. "But, if she doesn't turn up tomorrow, I'm afraid they'll have to be told. It's getting serious, Linda."

"I shouldn't worry too much," Linda said. "She's off on a binge with some of her gang and has just forgotten to tell you."

The telephone in the hall rang shrilly.

"I'll get it," Pat called over her shoulder. She picked up the receiver. "Hello?"

"Pat!"

"Johnny! Johnny Curtin! Of all the nerve..."

"Pat, *listen!* I can't explain now about the car, and I know you can't talk at that end. The reason I went off and left you ... well, it was on Gloria's account."

"Johnny! You know where — "

"Yes, Pat." Johnny's voice was very grave. "I know where she is. Look, you've got to come downtown right away ... Washington Place. Number 22B ... name of Bradley. Got that?"

"Yes, Johnny, but the family ... I mean they're having a little party, I — "

"You come, Pat! And listen, darling, things aren't very nice, I mean ... there's been an accident."

"Oh, Johnny!"

"You must come, Pat!"

"Yes, of course. Washington Place, 22B ... Bradley." She turned back to the kitchen, where Linda Marsh was just starting for the living room with the sandwiches. Pat's eyes were wide and frightened.

"Linda, that was Johnny. It was about Gloria. He says there's been an accident."

"Pat!"

"He didn't say what it was, but it's urgent. I don't want the family told. Tell them … tell them I forgot something at the Garden. I'll slip out the back way."

"Of course, angel," Linda said. "You don't want me to go with you?"

"Johnny's there," Pat said. She was already in the hall.

The sharpness in Linda's voice stopped her. "Pat, listen." She looked anxiously at the younger girl. "If anything has happened to Gloria, you'll let me know at once?"

"I will, Linda. Johnny didn't explain …" Pat was struggling into a coat.

"It's important," Linda Marsh said. "Because if something has happened to her I may be able to help."

"I know you would, Linda dear. But it's our mess."

"You don't understand, Pat. I've been afraid … afraid for almost two weeks that something would happen to her. Let me know at once, Pat. Promise!

"I promise," Pat said.

3

Mr. Julius twisted around from his position on the couch as the door of Bradley's apartment opened. Johnny Curtin, still wearing his overcoat, stood in front of the fire as though he were frozen. It was Bradley himself who came in. He dropped his hat and coat on a chair by the door.

"You telephoned Miss Prayne?" he asked Johnny.

"Yes. She's coming."

Mr. Julius stirred impatiently. "Well, damn it, what about it? Do we have to pry information out of you?"

Bradley was exploring his pockets. His mild eyes held an unaccustomed glint of anger.

"It's murder, right enough," he said quietly. "She was strangled to death with a silk scarf, presumably her own." From a red tobacco tin he began filling the bowl of a stubby black pipe. His gaze was on Johnny. "Why?" he asked.

"I … I don't get it."

"I'm asking you why she was killed!" Bradley said. "She's only a kid — twenty-three or four at the outside. From your account she comes from a decent family. She's not a gangster's moll or a harlot. She's not the kind of girl who dies this way."

"The Colonel's lady and that O'Grady person," Mr. Julius

said with a dry chuckle. "Don't ask this young fool about Gloria. He's all mixed up about her and her sister. He's all mixed up about the facts of life."

"Do you know why she was killed. Julius?" the inspector inquired.

"Certainly," said Mr. Julius.

"Why?"

"Because somebody hated her or she was dangerous to someone."

"Who?" Bradley's tone was resigned.

"How the devil should I know? That's your job."

Bradley shrugged and turned hack to Johnny. "They've taken the car to headquarters. Fingerprints...photograph the body before it's removed. Not that I expect them to find fingerprints after you and our friend here have climbed all over it."

"No use in it anyway," snapped Mr. Julius. "She wasn't killed in the car. Coat, gloves, purse thrown in on top of her. Killed somewhere else ... indoors. Body put in car afterward. Possessions dumped in helter-skelter."

"So you noticed that?"

"My eyesight is unimpaired." said the old man crisply. "How long's she been dead?"

"We'll have to wait for a report on that," said the inspector. "But it's been a good many hours a day or two perhaps."

"God!" Johnny said. Bradley eyed him, Johnny moistened his lips. "You see, Inspector, Gloria's been missing since Wednesday. Guy and I — that's Guy Severied to whom Gloria was practically engaged — have been hunting all over town for her for three days."

"Didn't a disappearance of that sort seem important enough to you or to her family to call in the police?"

Johnny looked down at his hat, which he was twisting round and round in his fingers. "Gloria was...well, sort of scatterbrained, Inspector. She used to run around a great deal — parties, friends everywhere. It wouldn't have been unlike her to go off and forget to notify anyone."

"Weren't her mother and father worried?"

"Her mother's dead, Mr. Bradley. The two girls live with their father and Miss Celia Devon, their aunt. Mr. Prayne and Miss Devon were told Gloria was staying with an old friend, Linda Marsh. Pat didn't want to say anything till she knew what Gloria was up to. Gloria got enough publicity as it was."

Mr. Julius had closed his eyes, looking for all the world as if he were asleep. He opened them now — bright, unblinking eyes like a bird's. "Gloria was a trollop!" he said, and closed his eyes again, resting his head against the couch.

Johnny blushed. Bradley waited. "She...she was a little wild," Johnny admitted. "Things were tough for her. The Praynes were lousy with money until Mr. Prayne's brokerage firm went phutt and they lost everything."

"So Douglas Prayne sat on his behind and whimpered. A weakling. Always said so and to his face," interrupted Mr. Julius without moving.

"It was Pat who took hold." said Johnny. "They had horses. She and George Pelham, an ex-cavalry officer, started a riding school. They teach people to jump...and school and sell horses on the side. Guy Severied, who is Pelham's best friend, put up the money to recondition an old loft building on Ninety-First Street and to meet expenses for a bit. They've made a go of it...paid Guy back. But it's still damned hard work, and not much profit. Gloria couldn't take it. She was used to having everything."

"Stuff and nonsense!" said Mr. Julius. "A trollop! Been chasing every eligible man with money in town. You know Severied. Polo...yachts."

"I've heard of him," said Bradley. "And what was your connection with Gloria Prayne, Mr. Curtin?"

Again Johnny looked down at the twisting hat. “I…I’m in the horse business, too, Inspector. Have a little breeding farm up in Millbrook. Pat came up there one day to look at a horse. I… well, I kind of fell for her. I started coming to New York to see her. We…we had a lot of fun. Pat is the grandest girl you ever met, Mr. Bradley.”

“About Gloria,” said Bradley gently.

The glow from the fire heightened the color that mounted in Johnny’s cheeks.

“Naturally, I met her,” he said. “She…she was colorful and…exciting.”

“Like a Christmas tree,” said Mr. Julius from behind his veiled eyelids. “Lot of glitter and tinsel…no roots.”

“I lost my head,” Johnny confessed. “I started giving Gloria a rush.”

“I thought she was engaged to Severied,” said the inspector.

“Not officially. I thought until it was official 1 had a right to…to see what I could do.”

“Then he found the apple had a worm in it,” chuckled Mr. Julius.

“I realized I’d been a dope, Inspector,” Johnny said. “I took Gloria to El Morocco last Wednesday night. I told her…how I felt. I told her I’d crawl back on my hands and knees to Pat if she’d have me. Gloria got sore and went away.”

“Couldn’t bear to lose a man…even if she didn’t want him,” said Mr. Julius.

“And that, so far as any of us knows,” said Johnny, “is the last time Gloria was seen by any of her friends until tonight.”

“Tonight?”

“When I opened the rumble seat to … to put Pat’s things in the back of the car.”

Bradley puffed thoughtfully on his pipe for a moment or two. His eyes studied Johnny, probing, weighing. Finally he said, “All right, Mr. Curtin. Let's go back over tonight. You were waiting outside the Garden by her car for Miss Patricia Prayne?"

"That's right. When she came out, she had a lot of stuff to go in the rumble. She gave me the keys and asked me to do it for her while she finished up in the Garden. I opened the rumble...." Johnny paused, and the corner of his mouth twitched. "I...saw Gloria...with that thing tight around her neck and her face black and horrible." He drew a deep breath. "I slammed it shut. I put Pat's stuff in front and drove straight to Mr. Julius' apartment on Eighth Street."

"Weren't there any policemen around?" Bradley asked.

"Yes. As a matter of fact, I gave one of them a dollar to give to Pat in case she didn't have taxi money."

"Didn't it occur to you to report to him what you'd found?"

Johnny's jaw set stubbornly. "I didn't want Pat mixed up in it. I know the police. Her car...a body in the back of it. I...Well, I didn't want her to go through that if I could help it."

"The poor, stupid police," murmured Bradley.

"Apt description!" Mr. Julius' eyes popped open. "Wonderful for directing traffic — there it ends. Blundering, blustering, bullying — that's the police. Pick on innocent citizens. Let crooks run the city. Humph!"

Bradley sighed. "And why did you go to Mr. Julius?"

Johnny frowned. "It ... it was instinctive. He's a sort of uncle of the Praynes, and he's often told us how he helped you with that stamp murder last year. He said you were...were reasonably intelligent." Johnny grinned.

"Mercy," said Bradley. "Praise from Caesar."

"Hope the build-up wasn't phony," said Mr. Julius. "You're not acting very spry at the moment."

Bradley ignored him, keeping his eyes on Johnny.

"So I went to Mr. Julius and told him what I'd found. We came here, and that's that."

"You realize," said Bradley, "that you're going to have to answer a lot of awkward questions? You were the last person to see Gloria Prayne alive…you were the person to find her. You deliberately withheld information from the police until it suited your convenience. You had quarreled with Gloria Prayne. Perhaps she stood in the way of a reconciliation with her sister."

"Bosh!" said Mr. Julius. "He did what any normal man would do to protect his girl. Wanted her to have a break. That's all. Stop being ponderous. Doesn't suit you. Bradley."

"Um," said Bradley. "Do you plan to take a hand in this, Mr. Julius?"

The old man looked belligerent. "Mean to see Pat is protected."

Bradley sounded hopeful. "Have you any fundamental interest in catching a particularly brutal murderer? Because that's my job, y'know."

"Naturally!" snapped Mr. Julius. "Just don't want to see you act like a bull in a china shop."

The doorbell rang. Instantly Johnny sprang across the room, "That'll be Pat,"

Bradley knocked out his pipe. "Sometimes I hate this job," he said.

They heard Pat's eager voice as Johnny opened the door, "Oh, Johnny! Where is she?"

"Hate it like hell," said Bradley.

Mr. Julius glanced up. For the first time there was a look of warmth in his faded blue eyes. "She's a thoroughbred, Bradley. Only one in the family with guts. Deserves a break. Do your best, won't you?"

Bradley smiled down at Mr. Julius. "You sentimental old hypocrite," he said, Then he turned to look at Pat, who was suddenly clinging desperately to Johnny. She had been told the news. Bradley's face sobered.

"I'll do my best for her," he said.

4

Mr. Julius rose. as Johnny led Pat to the couch. When she reached the old man, she buried her head on his shoulder and sobbed.

"Here! No use in tears!" Mr. Julius blustered. He glowered helplessly at Bradley. "Great Scott, I'm no hand at this sort of thing. Don't gape! Do something!"

Bradley went into his kitchenette and returned with a jigger of brandy and a glass of water. He handed them to Pat.

"Take it easy," he said. "Don't gulp."

Pat drank the brandy and then Johnny, hovering about, eased her down onto the couch. None of them spoke until the storm of emotion had subsided. "Somebody give me a cigarette," she said at length.

Johnny lit one himself and handed it to her. Her eyes avoided all their faces. "I suspected that s-she was dead, after what Johnny said on the phone. I…I was ready for that, Uncle Julius. But murder!"

"It's nasty!" said Mr. Julius. "'But don't try to carry the whole load yourself. Time your father faced some responsibility. Ducked for years. He can't duck murder!"

Pat's slim brown hands were laced together. "It's so stupid, so senseless! Gloria wasn't important! She had nothing anyone wanted! Why? Why should someone want to kill her?"

"I had hoped," said Bradley quietly, "that you might be able to tell me that, Miss Prayne."

"But I can't!" Pat cried. "I can't! She was wild, like a green colt. She did a lot of stupid things. But she hurt no one but herself."

"There has to have been a reason, Miss Prayne," Bradley said. "There always is. And the reason is sometimes harder to take than murder itself. But we have to go after it."

"Of' course," Pat said. "Of course we have to go after it. Every one of us has to go after it, because whoever did this has got to pay for it." She looked at Mr. Julius. "I've been so damned mad at Gloria so damned often, Uncle Julius. But this…"

"Let's get a few essential facts, Miss Prayne," said Bradley. His voice, cool and impersonal, checked the threat of further tears. "I have Curtin's story. He discovered your sister's body when he went to put your things in the back of the ear. He acted, somewhat unwisely and impetuously, to save you the shock of discovery. For the moment, at least, I'm accepting his story. So we come to the heart of this thing. How did your sister's body get in the back of that car, Miss Prayne?"

Pat stared at him. "But I haven't the faintest idea, Inspector. I —"

"Where has that car been since, say, Wednesday night, which was the last time any of you actually saw Gloria?"

"I've had it, Inspector," Pat said. "We've exhibited horses at the Show all week. I've driven to the Garden each morning about eight, for the exercise periods, and stayed there until the Show closed at midnight. The car's been outside the Garden all day … every day."

"Where?"

Pat looked down at her hands. “I don’t like to get anyone in trouble, Mr. Bradley. I …”

Bradley smiled. “Some cop let you park where you weren’t supposed to. That it?”

She nodded. “Outside the exhibitors’ entrance on Forty-Ninth Street.”

“Then you’re the only one who’s used the car all week?” It sounded casual enough.

“Don’t answer that, Pat,” Johnny Curtin said sharply. “Somebody put Gloria’s body in the car after Wednesday night. If you say — ”

“Please, Curtin, don’t pop off,” Bradley interrupted in a tired voice. “I’m trying to make it easy by questioning Miss Prayne here, with her friends about, instead of alone at headquarters.”

“But you’re trying to trap her,” Johnny protested.

“Shut up, Johnny,” said Mr. Julius. He was sitting on the couch beside Pat, his eyes closed again.

“This isn’t meant to be a trap, Miss Prayne,” Bradley said. “Someone at some time during the week put your sister’s body in the back of the car. Quite obviously it couldn’t have been done while it was parked outside the Garden. I’m trying to find out when it could have happened … and who had access to the car.”

Pat was frowning. “A lot of people used the car,” she said. “Someone was always having to run back to the school for something we’d forgotten. Peter Shea, our groom, used it; George Pelham … I don’t know who else.”

“You don’t know?”

Pat met the inspector’s eyes steadily. “The car keys were left on the table in the tack room,” she said. “Anybody could have borrowed them without our paying particular attention.”

“Don’t you see what that means, Inspector?” Johnny said. “Thousands of people were milling in and out of the Garden stables every day. Anybody … anybody in the whole of New York could have taken those keys and used the car. And there's no way to check."

Bradley looked down at Mr. Julius. An understanding glance passed between them.

"Don't be a fool, Johnny," said the old man. "We're dealing with a cold-blooded murderer. Someone who thought out a very neat way of getting a body off his hands after he'd killed. Anyone in New York? Phooey. Someone who knew, Johnny. Someone who knew where the car was, where the keys were. Someone who could take those keys and not create suspicion if he were caught at it."

Pat's lips began to tremble.

"No use beating around the bush," said Mr. Julius. "Somebody close … somebody intimate with your routine. That the way you see it, Bradley? Family … close friends?"

Bradley sighed. "I'm afraid so," he said.

5

JOHNNY stepped from the revolving door into the crowded entryway of the Blue Moon Club. The air was thick and stale, He could hear the dull. tom-tom thumping of a band and the shuffle of feet on the postage-stamp dance floor.

A hat-check girl tried to relieve him of his things.

"I'm not staying," he told her. "I'm looking for Guy Severied."

"The marines!" said the girl. "Boy, is Gus going to be glad to see you if you're a friend of Severied's. He's in at the bar."

Johnny pushed on into the blue-lit room beyond. After searching Tony's, The Famous Door, The Onyx, Leon and Eddie's, and a half dozen other places, if he didn't find Guy here he would go on to the Praynes' without him.

He had been at the Blue Moon before, with Gloria. Then he'd laughed at the murals, danced endlessly to the rhythms of Skinny Evans' band, and been trampled in the rush of Gloria's admirers. Nobody noticed him now as he worked his way toward the oval bar. It was too late in the evening to pay attention to anyone, even grim-faced young men who had somehow managed to get past the checkroom without giving up hat or coat.

Johnny saw Guy Severied. He was sitting on a high stool at the bar, and several men were standing by him. One was Gus, the Blue Moon's proprietor; one the headwaiter; the others were frowzy-looking red-eyed young men who seemed amused. Gus and his majordomo wore that glassy expression that comes over such people when they are having trouble with a valued customer.

"Drink for everybody in the place is what I said," Guy was saying. He spoke with a careful dignity.

"Sure, Mr. Severied, sure," Gus soothed.

"And I want 'em all set up on the bar…in a line. No trickery, Gus, my friend. Line 'em up."

There must have been five hundred people in the place. It was awkward. If Gus refused, Guy would be noisy and unpleasant. If Gus obeyed, Guy, sober, would raise hell when he got the bill.

Johnny came up and put his hand on Guy's arm. Guy flung it off and turned, eyes squinted to bring this new nuisance into focus.

"Well, as I live and breathe! Young Lochinvar!"

"I've got to talk to you, Guy."

Guy waved to include all his audience. "My first customer, Gus. You didn't know I was running a service for the lovelorn, did you?"

"No, Mr. Severied."

"Well, I am. Damn good service. Tell 'em what to do and they live happily ever after … if they live!" That he decided was very funny. Gus and the headwaiter smiled their frozen smiles of appreciation.

"Guy, I've got to tell you something privately," Johnny said.

"Positively not," said Guy. He brought one huge hand down

on the bar. Glasses bounced. Gus closed his eyes in pain. "I never, under any circumsha … circum*stance*, give advice after two in the morning. If a man doesn't know what to do after two in the morning, he doesn't need advice; he needs a doctor. Run away, Lochinvar."

"Come off it, Guy," said Johnny, his voice sharp.

"Oh," said Severied happily. "Trouble!" He slid to his feet.

"Take it easy, Mr. Severied," Gus pleaded.

Johnny didn't give an inch. His eyes were cold. "The hell with him," he said. "I'd just as soon take him out of here horizontal."

"Now, now, take it easy," said Gus again.

Guy looked sad, "Did she turn you down with an awful thud, Lochinvar? You mush … must have played your cards very badly. But really … no advice now. I wouldn't do justice to myself." He rested his hands heavily on Johnny's shoulders. "You wouldn't guess it, but the truth is I'm just a touch tight!"

"I don't want advice. I want to tell you something…now and in private."

Severied peered around the smoke-dimmed room. "Not built for privacy." Then his eyes lit up. "The washroom. Beautiful place. Air-conditioned. Never over a hundred an' ten in the shade. And lovely fans make a lovely noise…like," he explained musically, "'the dawn comes up like thunder, out of China 'cross the bay-ee!'" He took Johnny by the arm and started.

"Cigars? Cigarettes?" A girl with a tray stopped them, looking up at Guy.

"Certainly," said Guy. "I'll take a carton of Camels, a carton of Chesterfields, a carton of Luckies, a carton of …"

"For God's sake, come on," Johnny snapped. "Cut the comedy."

Guy beamed at the girl. “Later,” he said, and gave her a resounding whack on the rear as she passed. “Great place,” he said. “Gentleman’s club.”

They went down a steep flight of stairs. The washroom was small and, as Guy had predicted, hot as a furnace. Guy went to a washbasin, filled with lukewarm water, and began washing his hands.

“Listen, Guy,” Johnny said. “We’ve found Gloria.”

“In what opium den?” asked Guy, soaping his hands.

“Okay, pal, take it on the chin,” said Johnny. “She’s dead. Murdered.”

Guy spun around, lost his equilibrium, and fell back against the wall. He leaned there, his hands, held out in front of him,. dripping soapy water.

“That’s a hell of a way to sober a man up,” he said.

“It’s straight, you mug. She was strangled. I found the body in the rumble of Pat’s car. The police have sent me to find you. They want us all at the Praynes’ apartment.”

Guy shook his head, like a punch-drunk fighter. “Murder? Johnny, this isn’t a gag?”

“I wish it were, but…It’s the works.”

“Damn!” Guy dried his hands and glanced at the mirror. Then he pulled down his lower lids and looked at his bloodshot eyes. “What a mess,” he muttered. “This was meant to be a private binge, Johnny…strictly private…But, let’s go, Johnny. We got things to do.”

They were overwhelmed with assistance when they got back upstairs. The headwaiter whisked Mr. Severied’s coat and hat from the checkroom; Gus helped Mr. Severied into his coat; Gus would not hear of Mr. Severied’s writing a check for his bill; some other time. Mr. Severied’s credit was aces. Anything, in short, to get Mr. Severied rolling.

"I never saw him like this before," Gus whispered to Johnny. "He must of cleaned up at the races or something."

The doorman escorted Mr. Severied into a taxi.

"Ninety-first and Madison," Johnny said, and climbed in beside Guy.

"No!" Guy contradicted. "Twenty-one West Fifty-six…an' don't spare the horses."

"Ninety-first and Madison, driver."

The driver was patient. "Make up your minds, gents."

"You go where I told you," Guy said. "And if that isn't okay with you, young Lochinvar, you can always take another cab."

"Isn't that where Linda Marsh lives?" Johnny asked.

"On the nose," said Guy.

"She's not there," said Johnny. "She's with Pat, at the Praynes'."

"One will get you three she isn't."

"For God's sake, Guy, I tell you Linda's with Pat!"

The cab had stopped for a red light at Fifth Avenue. "Don't come if you don't want to," Guy said. "Change horses in midstream if yon want to."

Johnny shrugged and settled back himself. It was important to get Guy uptown. Bradley had played ball. He had given Pat a chance to break the news to her family alone. He had given Johnny the chance to find Guy without sending out an alarm. And apparently he had kept the news from the press so far.

Two minutes later they were at 21 West Fifty-sixth.

"Hold. it," Johnny told the driver, "we'll be going on." He and Guy walked into the foyer of the apartment building.

The night man regarded Guy, who was waving like a stately pine in a stiff breeze, with suspicion.

"Miss Linda Marsh," Guy said.

"Miss Marsh isn't in."

"Impossible. Call her apartment."

Johnny nodded to the night man. Anything to wheedle a drunk, his look said. The man plugged in a cord on the switchboard and held his finger down on a button.

"He's stalling," Guy accused. "I'll break his goddamn neck for that. He's stalling!"

"Ring the bell yourself, chief," said the man.

Guy rang it, long and vigorously. "Owe you an apology," Guy said. "If you feel it is an insult for which an apology will not suffice, I'll be glad to receive your seconds at the proper..."

"Guy! Let's go."

"Oh. Check."

They got into the cab again.

"Linda Marsh, Inc., Forty-fifth Street and Fifth Avenue," Guy ordered.

"Listen, dope," Johnny said, "it's after three! No one's at Linda's shop."

"Except Linda," said Guy.

Johnny's eyes measured the distance from his right fist to the point of Guy's jaw. "Look," he said. "If Linda isn't there, will you to the Praynes?"

"Word of honor," said Guy. "But she'll be there; that's a certainty, like the rising of the sun, or the...or the..." He subsided.

The taxi drew up behind a black sedan at the curb in front of Linda Marsh, Inc. Guy got out and moved under full sail toward the locked and bolted entrance of the dress shop. Johnny followed. He was halfway across the sidewalk before he heard the sedan door slam and someone came up behind him.

Johnny turned to face a man with a derby hat pulled down square on his bullet-shaped head.

"Okay, pals, what d'you want?" said the man.

Guy gestured to Johnny. "Give him a dime for his cup of coffee and tell him to scram."

The man's head seemed to sink between his shoulder blades like a turtle's. Then he exploded.

"I'm Sergeant Snyder of Homicide," he said, "and if you don't wanna cool your fanny in the hoosegow, start talkin'."

"Homicide? Connected with Inspector Bradley?" Johnny asked.

"You're damn right I'm connected with him. I'm his assistant."

"Oh. My name is Curtin."

"You the guy discovered the Prayne dame's body?"

"Right. This is Mr. Severied. I'm taking him to the Praynes', but he's got a notion that Miss Marsh is here and that he must see her first."

"Oh, Yeah? Well, she's here all right. But it'll be up to the inspector if anyone sees her. He's with her now."

Meanwhile Guy had been ringing the night bell. Johnny saw a light appear at the far end of the shop.

"How'd you know Linda was here, Guy?"

Guy looked wise. "Told you it was as certain as...well, certain, didn't I?"

"But how did you know?"

"I get around, young Lochinvar. I get around."

The door of the shop opened and Bradley stood there, pipe between his teeth, hands in the pockets of his trench coat. His eyes questioned Johnny.

"This is Severied, Inspector. He ..."

He broke off as Guy brushed past the inspector and made a beeline for the back of the shop, colliding only once with a sheet-covered counter.

"I'm sorry," Johnny said. "He's boiled to the ears."

"How did he take the news?" Bradley asked, watching Guy disappear into the office at the rear.

"He's too drunk to react to anything," Johnny said. "But he insisted he had to see Linda. The only way I could get him moving was to stick with him. How he knew she was here I can't tell you."

"I'd like to find out myself," said Bradley "Come on in."

"If you have any trouble with that monkey, Red, holler," said Sergeant Snyder.

6

IN THE setting Linda Marsh had designed for herself there was no hint of business. Johnny blinked at the thick rug, the deep chairs, the glowing fire. He noticed a magnificent Goddard desk and a tray on a table by the couch carrying glasses, a bowl of ice, and several bottles.

Johnny and the inspector were close enough on Guy Severied's heels to hear him ask Linda, "Have you given it to him yet?"

Linda was standing with her back to the fire, a green chiffon handkerchief stretched between her lingers. "Guy! Oh, my dear, then you know?"

"Have you given it to him?" Guy repeated.

"Not yet, Guy. But I must."

"Not necessarily." Guy wheeled, bracing himself on the back of a chair. "This is all rot," he said to Bradley. "Melodramatic rot. Just raise a stink and get you nowhere." In spite of a supreme effort he was swaying slightly.

"So you know about the letter, Mr. Severied?" Bradley said, his face thoughtful.

"Of course. Why else would I be here?"

"I'm just a stranger here myself," Johnny said angrily. "I've been dragged around by the nose for the last half-hour without being told why."

For the first time Linda looked at him. Her dark eyes grew warm. "Johnny, this has been dreadful for you. Pat told me."

"Forget it," Johnny said. "What the hell's going on? I thought you were with Pat. I counted on that. She shouldn't be alone."

"I was just about to get the answers to those questions myself," said Bradley, "when you arrived, Curtin. Suppose you begin again, Miss Marsh."

"Look," Guy said. "This is all rot, I tell you. Workings of an overdeveloped imagination. Just make trouble for innocent people. Go hunt clues, Inspector. Get out your magnifying glass and your bloodhounds, but forget about this. Gloria was nuts! Well, just ask any of her friends."

"You and Gloria Prayne were about to be married, weren't you, Mr. Severied? You should be able to tell us a good deal."

"Sure I could." Guy pressed fingers against his perspiring temples. "If I told you I was relieved when Lochinvar here brought me the news, I suppose you'd get out your handcuffs?"

"Are you telling me that?" Bradley's eyes were steady.

"Why not? I wasn't in love with Gloria…and Gloria wasn't in love with me. Mutual non-admiration society. Very funny, if it wasn't very unfunny. But Gloria loved yachts. Catch on?"

"Guy, you don't know what you're saying!" Linda protested.

"Always know what I'm saying. I hate to shatter the ideals of young Lochinvar, but all that glitters in the eye is not love. Easier to go through with it and work out some kind of a life afterward. Things were complicated."

"You're not going to confess to murder and save us a lot of trouble, are you, Severied?" Bradley's tone was hopeful.

Guy waggled a finger at him. "Now, now, Inspector. There are no short cuts to success."

"You damned drunkard!" Johnny blazed. "What the hell do you think this is, some kind of a game? Let's get to the point. Pat needs us...*some* of us, anyhow."

"Yes, Miss Marsh, let's get to the point," said Bradley.

Linda found her voice. "I was telling Mr. Bradley about a visit I had from Gloria two weeks ago," she said, addressing herself to Johnny. "I was explaining to him that I grew up with the Prayne girls...lived next door to them and all that; that they've taken the place of my own family."

"Known privately as 'the problem family,'" Guy put in. "Only one who ticks is Pat. Swell girl. Ever see her on a horse, Inspector?"

"Shut up," Johnny said.

"Sorry," Bradley said, "but how can I get it across that this is *my* party? Miss Marsh?"

"The day Gloria came to see me," Linda said, "she was nervous, almost incoherent. She talked about making the headlines one of these days. 'Feet first' was the way, she put it. She was afraid of someone afraid something was going to happen to her."

"Who was she afraid of? Did she say?"

"Pipe dream," Guy began.

"No." Linda ignored him. "Frankly, Inspector, I didn't take her very seriously. She loved to dramatize herself and she always exaggerated."

"Still you felt she was really frightened?"

"Yes. But it's difficult to explain."

"Take your time."

The green handkerchief was wound into a tight knot. "She was terrified, but I thought she was imagining the danger. There was no reason for her to be afraid of anyone."

"Check," said Guy. His voice had thickened. His eyelids drooped.

"I was too busy for any soul swabbing, even for Gloria," Linda said.

"And the purpose of her visit?" Bradley prodded her. "She wanted you to do something for her?"

"Yes. She had a letter with her, Mr. Bradley, in one of her own blue envelopes, sealed with wax, and no writing on it."

"No writing?" Guy's eyes opened. "Positively no writing?"

"That's right, Guy."

Guy crossed his fingers elaborately. "Must remember that. Excellent legal point."

"What about the letter?" Johnny said.

"She asked me to keep it and, if anything happened to her, to turn it over to the police."

"You agreed?"

"Yes. I took it, put it in my desk drawer, and forgot about it."

"Good God!" Johnny cried. "You had that letter for the last three days and you didn't say anything?"

"Smart girl," said Guy. "Very, very smart girl. Sense values."

"Damn you, Guy, *shut up!*"

"You know Gloria, Johnny," Linda said. "Even when I heard she was missing I didn't think it was serious."

"If you'd turned the letter over to the police, you might have prevented this thing!" Johnny insisted.

"I think not," said Bradley quietly. "I've had the medical examiner's preliminary report. He thinks Gloria's been dead for several days. She was probably killed" — and his eyes moved to Johnny's face — "not long after she left you at El Morocco on Wednesday night, Curtin."

"But, Bradley, that means ..."

"Gives a rather unpleasant picture of the killer, doesn't it?" said Bradley. "A man with no nerves. He kept a dead body concealed for at least two days before he transferred it to the Praynes' car tonight."

"I keep trying to explain why I haven't done anything before now," Linda said. "Gloria was always in some sort of a mess. The Praynes, Mr. Prayne especially, were very sensitive about it. It brought them publicity. Just now, when she and Guy were on the verge of getting married, they were particularly anxious to avoid any fresh scandal."

"Joke," Guy muttered.

"She'd been off on binges before, and I'd covered up for her," Linda finished, "by telling her father she was staying with me. Pat and I didn't want him to worry."

Bradley said, "But aren't we wasting time? The letter, Miss Marsh. From what you say it may contain the murderer's name."

"That is pure, unadulterated hooey," said Guy. "Listen ..."

"The letter," Bradley said.

Linda went to the desk and pulled out one of the small upper drawers. She brought a thick envelope to Bradley. It was as she had described it; blue, unaddressed, the flap secured by three blobs of purple wax into which a signet had been pressed.

Guy groaned. "Sealing wax! The old Miss Walker's touch!"

Bradley turned the letter slowly in his fingers. He glanced up at Linda. "Most women couldn't have resisted opening this," he said with a smile.

Her laugh was high. "I've told you, Inspector, it didn't seem important...not till Pat came home tonight with the news. Then I thought you should see it."

"Quite right," said Bradley. He took a penknife from his pocket and snapped open the blade.

"Wait," said Guy. "Now we come to my entrance line. I know what's in that letter, Inspector."

"Mercy," said Bradley.

"I know what's in it, and I know it won't do you any good. But it'll do harm. Gloria had a nasty mind...oh, very nasty,"

"We'll have a look, anyway."

"Hold everything. Word of honor, it's a false alarm. Nothing to help you, Inspector, but plenty to raise hell with innocent people. Throw it in the fire. Promise you won't lose. Be a decent thing to do."

"Mr. Severied, I am neither a publicity agent nor a reporter. If this letter, meant for the police, is not relevant to the case, that's that. You can burn it to your heart's content."

Guy looked down at his fingers. "Legal point," he reminded himself. "Oh, yes. How do you know it's meant for the police? No writing on it."

Bradley had already slit the flap at the top, leaving the seals undisturbed. He drew out three sheets of matching note paper, unfolded them, and stood staring for a time. Guy slumped into a chair, his legs seeming to grow weak under him. Bradley reversed the pages and examined the backs.

"Care to see?" he asked in a flat voice. He handed the pages to Linda.

"But, Inspector! This doesn't make any sense. They're blank!"

Guy sprang to his feet, knocked against the table where the drinks rested, and sent a glass shattering on the hearth. *"Nothing written on them!"* he shouted, and burst into wild laughter. "The little bitch!" he choked, dropping back into the chair. "She was bluffing! Oh, my God, she was bluffing!"

"Perhaps I'll have that drink you offered me," Bradley said, eying Severied calmly. "Scotch and water. No ice."

"Must we celebrate as soon as a murder's committed?" Johnny said. "I'm getting right out of here. Pat needs me."

"Not yet," said Bradley, without taking his eyes from Guy. His look was so intent that Guy was forced to raise his head. "You said you knew what was in that letter, Mr. Severied?"

"Wrong, Inspector. Oh, very wrong," said Guy. "I *thought*

I knew. I knew what Gloria *said* was in the letter. But blank pages!" He struggled to control another gust of laughter. "I will speak well of the dead, Inspector. She wasn't quite the little louse I thought she was. It was a gag."

Bradley took the glass Linda held out to him. "You didn't think this was a gag, did you, Miss Marsh?"

"No, Inspector. As I said, although I didn't take it seriously there was no doubt that Gloria *did.*"

"Did you tell anyone about this letter?"

"No."

"And it's been in that desk ever since she gave it to you?"

"Yes."

"The drawer wasn't locked?"

"No."

"Then plenty of people had access to it?"

"Why…I suppose so…My secretary…"

"And visitors…customers?"

"Well, not so good a chance, Mr. Bradley. They're not often left alone in here."

Johnny moved restively. "What are you getting at?"

Bradley shrugged. "This may not be the letter Gloria gave to Miss Marsh."

"You mean that somebody substituted those blank pages for the ones Gloria had written?"

"Without breaking the seals?" Bradley shook his head. "Not possible. But a complete substitution, yes. That would take about five unobserved seconds. Quite easy."

"You're off base, Inspector," said Guy. "It's all a magnificent, magnificent hoax, devised with all of Gloria's schoolgirl ingenuity."

Johnny snapped his cigarette into the fire. "God damn it, I've had enough," he said to Bradley. "Linda says Gloria was scared. Well, she had a right to be, didn't she? She's dead!"

"Very dead," complained Bradley.

"Then make Guy tell you what she was scared of!"

Bradley looked at Guy. "Well, Mr. Severied?"

"No dice, Inspector," said Guy with a grin. "Absolutely, positively no dice!" He pointed his finger at Bradley. "And don't try any third degree, my fine friend. I don't take Swedish exercises every morning for nothing."

"Where do you live, Severied?" Bradley asked unexpectedly.

"Long Island, Riviera, California, and East Sixty-third Street. Got a hole in the wall there with a change of clothes and a soft bed. Like to have you come and see me sometime, Inspector. Cozy little place."

"Thanks," said Bradley. "I'll probably make it soon." He turned to Johnny. "Curtin, I'm going to ask you to take him home."

"Listen, do you realize Pat's alone with a hysterical family?"

"I know. Miss Marsh and I are going there at once. But I want Severied seen home and into bed. And I want to be certain" — he glanced at his wrist watch — "that it takes at least half an hour."

"Will you tuck me in, Lochinvar? Will you sing lullabies to me?" Guy's speech was very thick now, almost unintelligible.

"Why choose me to be a wet nurse to a drunk?" Johnny was far from amiable.

Bradley grinned. "Because I can trust you to come straight to the Praynes' when the job's done. Mind you, be sure it takes half an hour. Don't leave him before that."

"If you weren't a friend of Uncle Julius', I'd tell you to go to hell! But okay."

Guy's legs buckled when he stood up so that Bradley and Johnny had to support him out of the shop, where Rube Snyder got them a cab. Between them the three men hoisted Guy into the corner seat.

Guy made little moaning noises as they drove uptown and

then east. Once he opened his eyes.

"You're a good kid … a great kid," he said.

"You've certainly been giving us a fine lousing," said Johnny.

"Extremely clever," said Guy. Then he scowled. "Take care of Pat, Lochinvar. Pick her up on your saddle and go back to the West where you came from. Hell to pay before this is over."

"You're telling me!"

"Tabloids, radio, gossips," Guy stumbled on. "Wait and see, Lochinvar. They won't even let the dead rest in peace."

"What the hell are you talking about?"

"Take Pat away. Ride off into the sunset." He made a sweeping gesture with a limp hand. "They can't stop you, Lochinvar. Got nothing on you kids. Let the rest of us stew in this mess."

"Guy, what do you know? Are you holding out on something that'll settle this?"

"Holding out? No. Jus' being very, very cagey."

When the taxi stopped, the driver helped Johnny get Guy into the building. There the elevator boy, whom Guy called "Mike," took over. Together Mike and Johnny led Guy into his elaborate hole in the wall. The living room was furnished with nautical flavor. There were barometers and compasses, a handsome ship's model on the mantel, cupboards built like ship's lockers. Bowed casements facing the East River might have been the outlook of a wheelhouse. In the bedroom Guy collapsed sidewise on the bed.

"Gosh, what a load!" Mike said. "Can you manage him?"

"I think so. And thanks."

Johnny removed Guy's shoes, undid his collar, straightened him out on the bed, and covered him with a quilt. He looked at his watch. Ten minutes before he could leave. He paced the room, drawing impatiently on a cigarette. At last he switched off the lights. Guy lay on the bed like a log, breathing noisily. Johnny hurried down to the street and hailed a cruising cab.

THE moment the apartment door slammed, Guy reached out and turned on the bedside lamp. He sat up, groaning. He rubbed his face and scalp vigorously. Then he got to his feet, wavered into the bathroom, and was sick, He drank several glasses of cold water and was sick again. His face still gray and damp with sweat, he went back into the bedroom. From a closet he took a tweed suit, a necktie, and a soft, dark-blue shirt. He managed to get into them, combed his hair, and walked unsteadily to the coat closet by the front door. A muffler, a heavy tweed overcoat, and a brown felt completed his preparations.

Then he, too, went out.

Mike's eyes bulged when he saw him.

"You goin' places, Mr. Severied?"

"What's it look like, Mike?" Guy's voice was quite clear, though rough with fatigue.

"Well, I'll be doggoned," said Mike. "I thought you was out for a month!"

Guy's smile was wry. "Marvelous recuperative powers, we Severieds."

"Maybe you're goin' huntin' again, Mr. Severied?"

"That's right."

"Ducks? Gee, it must take guts to get out into them blinds when its so damn cold and wet … and dark."

Guy's fingers shook as he lit a cigarette. "Not ducks, Mike. Something much more exciting. A manhunt!"

"A *man*hunt!"

"That's right, Mike. You ought to try it sometime. The results are so unpredictable."

Mike shot a glance over his shoulder. Drunk after all! "Shall I call a cab for you, Mr. Severied?"

"No, thanks."

Mike watched him go, shaking his head.

7

CAPTAIN George Pelham opened the door of the Praynes' apartment to Johnny. His lined face was yellow, and his eyes looked like holes cut in a blanket.

"Oh, it's you, Johnny."

"Where's Pat?" Johnny asked as he draped his overcoat on a bench by the door.

"In Gloria's room with the inspector," Pelham said. "You've been with Guy?"

"Yeah. God, is he stinko!"

The corner of Pelham's mouth twitched, and he tried to cover it by pulling at the end of his mustache. "Nasty mess," he said.

"How are the others taking it?"

Pelham lifted his shoulders. "The old man folded, as might be expected. Celia and Linda are trying to bring him around so he can talk to the inspector. What about Bradley, Johnny?"

"Seems a good sort," Johnny said. "He could have put the heat on Guy, but he didn't." Exasperation spread across his face. "Guy acted crazy … as if he knew the answers and just wouldn't give."

"When he gets drunk he gets drunk," Pelham said.

"Maybe that's it. I've got to find Pat."

He went down the corridor to Gloria's bedroom. There he found Pat; Mr. Julius, who had brought her home; and Bradley. Pat went to him wordlessly, a dazed, hurt look in her eyes. He slipped an arm around her shoulders and held her close.

"Chin up," he whispered.

Over the top of her head he saw Mr. Julius. The old man was staring around Gloria's room with an expression of distaste. The pale-blue curtains, the canopied bed, the ruffled chaise lounge, the mirrored dressing table with its jars and bottles all came under his disgusted scrutiny. The air was heavy with some musky perfume.

By the windows, over which the curtains had been drawn, Bradley sat at Gloria's fragile Florentine desk. He gave Johnny a quick smile.

"Mercy, you're promptness itself. Thirty-eight minutes to the second. Have any trouble with the patient?"

"He's out like a light," Johnny said. "Anything new?"

"Only this." Bradley indicated a pigeonhole full of blue note paper and a brass pen tray. In the tray were a stub of purple sealing wax and a gold signet ring.

"No doubt of it," said Mr. Julius, "the letter was prepared here."

"Which letter?" Bradley asked, without looking at him.

"Damned childish habit of being cryptic," snapped Mr. Julius.

"There's nothing cryptic about it," said Bradley. "The seals on Miss Marsh's letter haven't been tampered with. If there was a substitution, and it seems likely, it was a complete job … envelope and all. Definitely two letters — the one Gloria wrote and the one the murderer prepared."

"The murderer!" Pat exclaimed.

"Who else?" asked Bradley. "Miss Prayne, either your sister

was playing a joke — bluffing as Severied said — or she wasn't. Miss Marsh doesn't think she was. I don't think she was. She was afraid, and her fears were certainly justified. I think she wrote a letter, telling who she was afraid of and why."

"But ..."

"The murderer somehow learned about the letter. He had to get rid of it. If he stole the letter from Miss Marsh's desk, it might be missed. In that case Miss Marsh would have told your sister, and Gloria would have rewritten her evidence and been more cautious about where it was left. So he substituted a second letter, outwardly a duplicate of the original."

"Been planning this for days," said Mr. Julius.

"Waited for just the right minute ... then blooey!"

Johnny felt Pat shiver. "That means," she said, "that he was at the Garden tonight, and that he's been at Linda's — in her private office — sometime recently."

"And here," said Bradley.

"Naturally," Mr. Julius said.

"Why here, Inspector? No one could ..."

Bradley cut her short. "Miss Prayne, he had to come to this room. He had to get at this particular letter paper, this wax, and this ring."

"Pat, you can't get away from it," Mr. Julius said. "Every step in this thing draws the circle tighter around your own group."

"Aren't you both jumping at conclusions?" Johnny said, responding to the entreaty in Pat's eyes. "Guy knew about the letter beforehand, and he seemed positive Gloria had been bluffing. This second-letter theory is no more than that, Bradley ... a theory."

"Mr. Severied was anxious for us to believe that," said Bradley. "Much too anxious."

"It's crazy even to think it was one of us," Pat broke in. "People are always in and out of the house."

“What people?” Bradley asked. “What people in the last two weeks?”

“A fair question,” conceded Mr. Julius.

Bradley glanced up at him and away.

“Well, there’s Father and Aunt Celia and myself, of course. Linda’s in and out often; Johnny’s been about; George Pelham’s is here nearly every day; and Guy, of course. And those are the ones who couldn’t have done it.”

“And the ones who could?” asked Bradley.

“Well, there’s Peter Shea, our groom. I sometimes send him up for something. But, of course, he couldn’t have done it either. And Melissa.”

“Who’s Melissa?”

“She’s a colored cleaning woman who comes in once a week. But it’s silly to consider her.” Pat’s face was flushed.

“I’m still waiting for the ones who could,” Bradley said.

“Well … you see I’m not home much during the day, Inspector. And this last week … the Show …” Her voice trailed off.

“Friends of Gloria’s?” Bradley suggested

“Gloria didn’t ask many friends here, Mr. Bradley. She was … well, she thought of the school as a sort livery stable. She usually met them other places.”

Bradley sighed. “The ones who could,” he repeated.

“But you simply can’t …” Pat said. Her fingers tightened on Johnny’s arm. “Aunt Celia or Father will be able to tell you.”

“But you don’t know of anyone except the people you’ve mentioned?”

“Yes, I do!” Pat said triumphantly. “Dr. Englehardt came to see Father about his arthritis.”

“I see,” said Bradley gravely.

“That’s Jarvis Englehardt,” Mr. Julius said. “New-fangled ideas of diet and injection. Suspect a lot of patients have died..

But murder!" He shrugged.

Pat's lips were trembling. "Mr. Bradley … I love these people we've talked about. I'd trust them with my life. Accusing one of them is unthinkable … *and I won't think it!* You've missed something somewhere, Inspector—something that would take you completely away from this line of suspicion. There has to be something."

Bradley regarded her gloomily for a moment. "I hope so," he said, "for your sake."

Johnny said, "Hasn't Pat been through enough, Bradley? Can't you get on without her now?"

Bradley didn't answer. He got up from the desk chair, crossed the room, and slid open the closet door. There were dozens of day dresses, evening dresses, several tailored suits, furs, and scores of pairs of shoes and slippers. He rummaged among the clothes on the hangers. Presently he turned to Pat.

"Miss Prayne, had your sister any private source of income?"

"No."

"I have a report from headquarters here," he said. He took a paper from his inside pocket. "Gloria was wearing an evening dress … new; silver foxes and a sapphire ring. For a girl whose family is supposed to be broke that's fancy equipment. And this …" he added, gesturing toward the closet.

"But," Pat explained, "Linda is in the dress business. She gave Gloria a lot … and always let us buy from her at cost."

"Another peculiar thing," Bradley said. "The labels had been cut out of the clothes she wore."

"That looks like an attempt on the murderer's part to keep her body from being identified," said Johnny.

"And then," said Mr. Julius, "he hid the body in her own car! When I was your age, Johnny, I used my brains for thinking!"

Johnny reddened and was silent.

"Also," said Bradley, "the labels are gone from most of the things in that closet. Why?"

Pat shook her head.

"How much did your sister have for clothes?"

"Why … about a hundred a month, I think, for everything."

"Could she have acquired that wardrobe, even at cost prices, for that?"

"I … I don't suppose she could."

"Pat … Good Lord, stop stalling!" commanded Mr. Julius. "Admit it's queer. But you don't need a crystal bell, Bradley. Gullible family … told clothes came from Linda, wanted to believe it, accepted it. She cut out the labels in case anyone happened to go through her things."

"And where *did* she get them?" Bradley asked.

"Do I have to spell it out for you? She was engaged to one of the richest men in America. Guy bought 'em."

"Of course that's it." Pat was eager. "There's nothing incriminating in Guy having bought her clothes, is there, Mr. Bradley?"

Bradley had taken the red tin from his pocket. "Probably not," he said absently. He filled his pipe. "I'm afraid I can't put off talking to the rest of your family any longer, Miss Prayne. Will you and Curtin get them together for me? Julius and I will be along in a moment."

"Well," said Mr. Julius, when they were alone, "what's eating you?"

Bradley waited till he'd gotten his pipe drawing properly. His eyes kept traveling around the scented, frilly room. "This family is broke, according to all reports," he said. "At least comparatively broke. Yet Gloria had every luxury."

Mr. Julius wrinkled his nose. "Place smells like a bawdy house!"

Bradley's grin was fleeting. "A revealing comment, Julius.

Wouldn't have believed it of you."

"Rubbish!"

"And speaking of smells," said Bradley, "when you've been in this business as long as I have, you get so that you can smell certain types of crime."

"Can't abide lectures. Don't believe in instinct," said Mr. Julius.

Bradley looked at him, unsmiling. "What does the average citizen do when he thinks his life is in danger?"

"Runs like hell," said Mr. Julius.

"Yes. To the nearest police station for protection."

"Unless he doesn't like policemen."

"Precisely."

"Stop being cute!" Mr. Julius' irritation gave his voice a rasping quality.

"People don't like policemen when they have something shady in their own lives. A man wouldn't ask for help if by explaining *why* he was in danger he incriminated himself."

"So?"

"So Gloria Prayne didn't ask for help."

"What kind of hogwash are you talking? Gloria was a fool — a frivolous, irresponsible idiot. But not a criminal."

"Gloria didn't tell Linda Marsh why she was afraid. She left evidence that would implicate the murderer only *after* she was dead!" Bradley sighed. "I'd like to bet that she herself told the murderer where she'd left that letter."

The old man glared. "Stick to facts."

"Blackmail is a nasty business," said Bradley.

"Blackmail!"

"Isn't it obvious? Clothes ... jewels ... furs. Taking no chances on her family's finding out where they came from."

"But I tell you Severied —"

"Why hide it?" Bradley asked, "Is there anything shameful

about taking presents from your intended husband? I think, Julius, that Gloria was blackmailing someone for this trousseau. The victim got restless, made threats. Gloria, frightened, wrote down his secret and left it with Linda. She told her victim to keep him from getting tough. But he outsmarted her. I think he got a look at the letter, prepared a duplicate, planted it. Then he was free to act. And he did … decisively."

"By heaven, got to admit it makes sense!" Mr. Julius said. Then he laughed. "But you've tied yourself up in knots. If the murderer was a blackmail victim and it wasn't Severied, then it wasn't someone in this intimate family circle. No one else has two thin dimes to rub together. Better decide which theory you like, Master Mind. You can't have 'em both!"

Bradley's eyebrows rose. "You think not?" he said.

8

THE PRAYNE family and their friends, with the exception of Guy Severied, were in the living room when Bradley and Mr. Julius came in. Bradley knew them all but Douglas Prayne.

The inspector's eyes went first to the dead girl's father, who was in his armchair by the grate. He looked frail and tired, his skin the color of alabaster, his eyes squinted as if the light were painful. Miss Celia Devon, her lips compressed, rocked back and forth opposite her brother-in-law. Steel needles on which she was knitting a dark-blue sock flashed and clicked in her fingers.

"Well, Lieutenant, do you know anything we haven't already been told?" she asked.

"Not a great deal," said Bradley cheerfully.

Johnny and Pat sat side by side on the couch. George Pelham stood by the sideboard, highball glass in his hand. He seemed to be trying to read on Bradley's face the answer to some secret question.

"I've told them about the letter," said Linda Marsh, "and why I failed to do anything about it sooner." She was seated in a wing chair, her head tilted back, the full skirt of her black dinner dress spread out around her. For a moment Bradley's eyes lingered there, almost against his will.

"While the subject is fresh in your minds," he said, moving farther into the room, "perhaps we can simplify things. We have come to certain tentative conclusions. One, that the murderer must have visited Miss Marsh's office during the last two weeks. If those of you who haven't been to the office will tell me now ..." He looked around the ring of tense faces. The fire settled in the grate, and in the curious silence it sounded like an avalanche.

"I don't know whether it's worse luck for you or for us, Lieutenant," said Celia Devon. "Linda gave a cocktail party at her office last Friday ... the night before the Horse Show opened. We were all there."

"And about fifty others," said Johnny.

Bradley rubbed the faint bristle on the side of his jaw. "It isn't hard to reconstruct the second phase," he said. "The disposal of the body, I mean. The murderer knew the time Miss Prayne would be riding in the Jumping Championship tonight and that everybody connected with her would be at the ringside, watching. He could slip down to the tack room and take the car keys without being seen. He did, and drove the car to the place where he had hidden the body, put it in the rumble, and came back to the Garden."

Douglas Prayne covered his eyes with a hand on which heavy blue veins stood out.

"It was easy to return the keys," Bradley went on. "The tack room must have been crowded. Almost easier to return them than to take them. Now, obviously, the murderer had to be at the Garden tonight. You were all there. The murderer also had to have visited Miss Marsh's office. You have all done that. And, finally, the murderer must have had access to this apartment. You all qualify for that, too. But in this last instance outsiders are almost nil. Miss Prayne says there was your groom, a cleaning woman, and Dr. Englehardt."

"Jarvis Englehardt!" said Celia Devon. "How thoroughly comic!"

Bradley's eyes rested on her flying fingers. "Can you tell us of any other visitors in the last two weeks. Miss Devon?"

"I take it you include Linda, Guy, Johnny, and George in your little home grouping," she said. "In which case, I cannot think of anyone else … excepting, of course, Jarvis Englehardt." She smiled thinly to herself. "Just what are you driving at, Lieutenant?"

"He's telling you very politely," snapped Mr. Julius, "that one of this precious bunch is a murderer. And he is an inspector, not a lieutenant."

Douglas Prayne roused himself. "We are fortunate to have you in charge, Mr. Bradley," he said. "Julius has spoken of you so often. And of your discretion."

"Thank you," said Bradley. "My job, however, is to lay a particularly brutal murderer by the heels." His glance circled the room.

"Of course," Douglas Prayne said quickly. "I want to apologize for not having put myself at your disposal the moment you arrived. But you will appreciate what this dreadful business means to me … to my family. I … well, I'm no longer young, Inspector."

"I quite understand," said Bradley.

"Having someone less friendly to deal with the situation could be very dangerous to all of us."

"Dangerous!" Bradley looked up. "You recognize there *is* danger, Mr. Prayne?"

"Certainly I do," said Douglas Prayne. "You see, sir" — and he lifted a pale hand — " the Praynes have come upon evil times. My business … then this. I know what this kind of thing can do to people's lives."

"Oh?" said Bradley.

"There will be reporters, photographers ... prying, snooping. Our privacy, our human- rights, our future happiness are in your hands, Bradley."

A strange, choking noise came from Mr. Julius' throat, and he turned and walked to the far end of the room. Bradley remained looking at Douglas Prayne with something like clinical interest.

"In your investigations," said Prayne, "you will naturally unearth a great many facts about us. I urge you, Inspector, to keep them private unless they have some vital connection with the case."

"What sort of facts?" Bradley asked. His voice was cold.

Prayne stirred restlessly in his chair. "Well, sir, my business has failed. At the moment I am in the awkward position of being supported by my daughter Patricia."

"Father!" Pat said.

"I still have important deals pending, Inspector," said Prayne. "If the gravity of my finances was made public ... well when a man's down, you know, people are inclined to kick him. That's human nature. So, if it's possible, I feel I have a right to keep my present position to myself."

Bradley did not reply.

Celia Devon's fingers were still. "An interesting point of view, don't you think, Inspector?"

"Then, of course," said Douglas Prayne, "there's Gloria."

"Yes," said Bradley, "there is certainly Gloria." He looked at Pat. The girl had taken her eyes from her father, and her cheek touched the sleeve of Johnny's dinner jacket.

"Gloria was harum-scarum, Inspector ... always getting herself involved in ... well, unpleasantnesses. You will come across these matters. Need they be made public?"

"Mr. Prayne, it is not my job to supply the newspapers with gossip. What they get will have to come from you or your family and friends."

"Thank you. Thank you very much," said Prayne.

"Is that all you wanted to say to me, Mr. Prayne?"

"Why, yes … I think it is."

"You haven't any information that will help us to discover your daughter's murderer?"

"Good God, no!"

"You're positive? You know of no one who was her enemy? No one who might benefit by her death?"

"Gloria didn't have anything to leave anyone!" Prayne objected.

"I wasn't thinking of money," said Bradley. "I wonder if you've quite taken this in, Prayne. Your daughter has been murdered, deliberately and in cold blood."

"My dear fellow!" It was a protest against a piece of bad taste.

"Nuts!" said Mr. Julius suddenly, from the end of the room.

"You must get the situation clearly, Prayne," Bradley said. "The murderer had a reason for killing, and he doesn't mean to be caught. If any of you know anything that menaces him, you are, yourselves, in real danger."

"I don't think I follow you," said Douglas Prayne.

"If any of you can help me, do it now before the killer has a chance to silence you. If you keep it back … if you yourselves decide what is important to tell me and what is not … *you may never get the chance.*"

Douglas Prayne sat up. "You mean we are in actual physical danger?"

"You are. If you're withholding information."

"But good God, man, we certainly have a right to protection!"

"You'll get what I can give," said Bradley. "But I cannot have men following you about from room to room in your home. And your danger lies here. Here in this house! Here among your friends!"

Pat Prayne spoke up angrily. "Mr. Bradley, you can't go on with the insane theory that one of us is a murderer. You've overlooked something … missed something."

Bradley held her look. The sympathy that should have been in his eyes was not there. "Something I haven't missed," he said. "Your sister was calling on someone. She had settled down in a chair or on a couch. Sitting relaxed and unafraid, just as Miss Marsh is at this moment! She had thrown off her coat. Her host went out of the room, perhaps to mix a drink. When he came back, he walked up behind her. She was wearing a silk scarf around her throat. Her friend leaned over her, took hold of that scarf, and yanked it tight. She struggled. I can see her hands tugging desperately at the noose. I can see her face turning dark … her eyes protruding … I can see her — "

"Stop it!" George Pelham shouted. "For Christ's sake!" He took a step toward Bradley. The highball glass slipped with a thud to the thick carpet as he sank into a chair and buried his face in his hands, his shoulders shaking.

Then Linda Marsh was across the room. She dropped on her knees and put an arm around him.

"George! Darling! You mustn't let it throw you! You mustn't!"

Bradley looked back to Pat. "I'm sorry, Miss Prayne. I want you to see why I can't give up simply because the people involved are your family and your friends. I want you to see why *you* mustn't build a wall around them."

After an instant Celia Devon said, in her dry, cutting voice, "I had no idea the police were so talented. The stage has lost a superb actor, Inspector."

"But I bow to the talent of the murderer, Miss Devon. I talked with him tonight, yet I have no notion of his identity."

"Inspector," Douglas Prayne interrupted, "if there's a

murderous maniac here, you must protect us. It's your duty."

Bradley's eyes fastened on Prayne. "If you care for your safety, Prayne, give me the facts. Facts about these people and their relationship with Gloria."

"But I have told you everything I know. The whole thing is incomprehensible to me. I can't ..."

He was stopped by the sharp ringing of the telephone. Pat went to the handset on a side table.

"If it's reporters, Pat, say nothing!" said Prayne.

Pat had picked up the receiver and answered in a flat voice.

"For you, Inspector."

Bradley took it from her. "Yes. Yes, Monahan. *What!* Well, where the devil are you now? ... Yes. Well, how do you like that for apples! ... Uh—huh ... Go back to the starting point and wait there. That's your only bet. If you make contact, call me here, my place, or headquarters."

He put the phone in its cradle. Everyone was eyeing him. "I thought you told me," Bradley said to Johnny, "you left Severied passed out cold?"

"I did."

"Well, he went out ten minutes after you did. And was sober enough to give one of the smartest tails on the force a complete run-around. He's skipped."

"Well, I'm damned!" said Johnny. "If he wasn't out like—"

"Any of you an idea where Guy Severied would be likely to go at this time of night?" Bradley snapped, looking from one to the other.

Something that passed for a laugh came from Celia Devon's tight lips. "When you've known us longer, Inspector, you will lose some of your refreshing optimism. Or have you already begun to notice a faint lack of co-operation?"

9

GEORGE PELHAM slipped from under Linda's arm and stood up. He stood very straight, with the ramrod back of an ex-cavalry officer.

"You have made grave charges against us, Bradley," he said. The nerve beside his mouth would not stop twitching, and he kept fiddling with his mustache as camouflage.

"I haven't made any charges against anyone." Bradley was calm again. "I have shown you the situation — one that should make you realize that this is no parlor charade."

"But a quick solution would be quite a feather in your cap!"

If Bradley was angry, he didn't show it. "There are two unfortunate facts about murder, Captain Pelham. You always have a murderer. And he can only hang once."

"Are you trying to frighten us?" Pelham said.

"Not at all, Captain. I had hoped to make it plain that it would be a feather in my cap if I solved this thing before someone else walked stubbornly into death."

"And does that give you the right to browbeat and intimidate us?"

"Mercy," said Bradley, "have I been browbeating you?"

"We are all very delicately adjusted, Inspector," said Miss Devon. "We have nerves, and it is very unkind of you to play on them."

"Shut up, Celia!" said Pelham. "It's time we understood our position. Are you going to make an arrest tonight … or rather, this morning, Bradley? Because it is morning. It's after four."

"There will be no arrest," said Bradley, "unless one of you chooses to give."

He looked hopeful.

"Give!" snorted Mr. Julius. "The only person in this outfit who ever gives anything, Bradley, is Pat, The rest are takers!"

"Julius!" Douglas Prayne's indignation was feeble.

Pelham went on doggedly. "Because if you've no evidence against anyone and you're not proposing to arrest me, I'm leaving."

Bradley looked about mildly. "I see no storm troopers guarding the doors, Captain. If you have no information to give me, I haven't much interest in what you do or where you go."

Pelham seemed taken back. "You don't insist on my staying?"

"Right, Captain. Of course, I could ask you if you know who murdered Gloria Prayne."

"Naturally I don't."

"I could ask you if you saw anyone borrow the car keys from your tack room at the Garden."

"I didn't."

"I could ask you if you put that substitute letter in Miss Marsh's desk or saw anyone else do it?"

"Of course not."

"And you don't know where I could find the interesting Mr. Severied?"

"Don't go off half-cocked about Guy," Pelham warned. "Perhaps he doesn't like police persecution either."

"You see, Inspector," said Celia Devon, "how touching is everyone's grief over Gloria's tragic death and how deep is our concern to lend every assistance in avenging it."

"My dear Celia," said Prayne, "I hardly think this is a moment to appreciate your witticisms."

Miss Devon gave her brother-in-law a hard look. "I wasn't aware, Douglas, that I had said anything even remotely amusing."

"Can I see you home, Linda?" Pelham asked.

Linda glanced at Bradley. "If the inspector doesn't need me any longer."

"All right, Miss Marsh. We'll give up for now. Some quiet reflection may help you all decide that it would be the course of wisdom and safety to play on my team. Good night."

Pelham and Linda went out together, the captain still looking a little deflated.

The rest of them remained uneasily where they were, waiting for a move from Bradley. At last Celia Devon put down her sock, which had advanced materially in the last half-hour.

"Are you fond of coconut layer cake, Inspector?"

Bradley's face broke into a grin. "With milk?"

"With milk," said Celia Devon.

"Miss Devon, I love you!"

"Then come into the kitchen." She was already on her way. "I believe that is the traditional setting for romantic policemen."

"Julius should make an excellent chaperon," said Bradley.

"Julius is going home!" said Mr. Julius. "I had intended to supply you with a little biographical material, but Celia will probably do a good job. And enjoy it," he added maliciously.

"It's too bad, Julius," said Miss Devon, "we can't involve you in this affair. I should relish seeing you squirm."

"After observing the reactions in this house," said Mr. Julius, "I've done enough squirming to last me a long time, thank you.

Good night!" He looked at Bradley pityingly. "The police have gone soft along with the rest of society. If I'd been you I'd have sweat the bejeesus out of this mob!" He stalked out into the hall, and a moment later the front door banged.

***

Douglas Prayne retired to his room. Pat and Johnny stayed huddled on the couch, talking in low voices. Bradley sat on the kitchen table, swinging his legs, and holding a badly damaged piece of layer cake in one hand and a glass of milk in the other.

"Like it?" asked Miss Celia Devon. She stood opposite him, an apron over her black lace dress.

"Wunnerful," said Bradley indistinctly.

"Made it myself," said Miss Devon. "Surprising what talents one discovers when it becomes necessary."

Bradley swallowed enough of his cake to become articulate. "Don't discover that you're a detective at heart, Miss Devon. I have trouble enough with my trained assistant. Monahan, for instance. Imagine his letting that souse get away!"

Miss Devon sat down in a plain chair by the table. "I owe you an apology," she said.

"So?"

"Accusing you of acting," said Miss Devon. "We all do to an extraordinary degree. We develop a mental picture of the person we'd like to be, and then try to behave like that person. Only when we come up against a crisis like this does the paint wear thin. Sometimes what shows through is not pleasant. Take me, for example."

"What's your picture of yourself, Miss Devon?"

"Cool, competent, witty, utterly self-sufficient," said Miss Devon without hesitation. "Marvelous powers of analysis. But if you scrape off the paint …" She shrugged. "I'm a sour, disappointed old maid, Mr. Bradley, irked by the fact that I have no family of my own and have to take care of this one. Any wit that I possess is not kindly. I make wisecracks to varnish an unflagging self-contempt for having allowed myself to drift into the situation here."

"Do you have other revelations?" Bradley asked.

"Quantities. Take my precious brother-in-law. He sees himself as a country gentleman, a man of affairs — a 'fine figure of a man,' as we used to say. Actually he has the spine of a jellyfish. He's never done a lick of real work in his life. He schemes and twists to find easy ways to get what he wants. He gets what he wants sometimes. There were easy ways back in the twenties, Inspector. His greatest fear is that his friends at the University Club will learn the truth about him. You must have seen all that for yourself."

Bradley nodded. "It was something of a shock."

Miss Devon's eyes softened. "Pat's the one person who's more than skin-deep. She's just exactly what she appears to be. Generous, honest, hardworking, loyal till it hurts. That young lummox in there isn't half good enough for her."

"What about him?"

"Not very complex, Inspector. He's been confused. Now he imagines he knows what it's all about. He's going to be desperately on Pat's side. If she fights you, Inspector, and I think she will as long as you persist in your charming belief that one of us is a strangler, he'll be with her. Probably be quite a nuisance. More cake?"

"Thanks." Bradley watched her cut another generous portion. "What about Pelham?" he asked.

"George? High-strung, neurotic, bitter — all this hiding a real sentimentality and kindliness underneath."

"What turned him sour?"

Miss Devon carefully brushed crumbs from the surface of the table. "Some people are better able than others to take the bumps in life, Mr. Bradley."

Bradley grinned at her. "So you've joined the obstructionists' club, too," he said.

"Obstructionists' club?"

"Look, Miss Devon, policemen have a way of remembering nasty things longer than the average mortal. Captain Pelham has been in the news before. I recall it very well, although it has nothing to do with my department."

"Oh, that!" said Celia Devon.

"Uh-huh."

"It would be pretty cruel to reopen that old case again, inspector."

"Investigating murders is not a kid-glove profession. As I recall it, Pelham's wife walked out on him five years ago … disappeared … no one was ever able to find out where she went or why. Suppose you tell me about it from the point of view of an insider."

Miss Devon shrugged. "Perhaps it may help to explain George's attitude," she said. "George was truly in love with his wife. She was beautiful, gay, a grand horsewoman. George went off on a business trip that spring. When he came back from that trip, Dorothy was gone."

"Walked out?"

"I didn't say that, Mr. Bradley. I said she was gone, disappeared, evaporated. She took no clothes, no money, left no message. Nobody has ever heard of her since."

"That much I knew."

"Of course George went to the police, and there was a lovely uproar in the papers. George offered rewards. The poor devil was almost out of his mind. In the end the police dropped the case. They never found a shred of evidence."

"And that was that?"

"Not at all. George turned to private detectives. He spent

every cent he had, and then Guy Severied began to foot the bills. Finally even the private detectives were ashamed to accept any more fees. The case of Dorothy Pelham was closed."

"Tough on Pelham."

"It was. He went to pieces — drink, nerves. He couldn't get on his feet; his business was gone. If it hadn't been for Guy, he'd probably have blown his brains out. They'd gone to college together, been in the Squadron at the same time. Theirs is about as close and loyal a friendship as you'll find in this cynical age."

"That was five years ago," said Bradley, groping for his pipe. "You said it might explain an attitude?"

"Because for the last few days I've noticed George had the jitters again. Tonight I realized they were due to Gloria's disappearance. They kept it from me and Douglas, but George knew. Don't you see what it must have done to him, Inspector? It was so like Dorothy's vanishing act. Gloria took no clothes, no money, and left no message. If George behaves queerly, Inspector, it's because this has reopened a wound that never really healed."

The line between Bradley's eyebrows deepened. "It's rather extraordinary, Miss Devon. Two vanishing ladies!" He struck a match, "I don't believe in coincidence," he added casually. "Do you?"

"I wondered if you would," she said without looking up. A cloud of blue smoke floated toward the ceiling. "How did Pelham happen to go into this school with Miss Prayne?"

"That was Guy's doing. When Douglas failed, Pat decided to start a school. Horses were something she knew. She went to Guy to see if he'd advance her the capital. He agreed — largely because, I think, he saw a chance for George. George is wonderful with horses. If he got interested, he might pull himself together."

"And it worked "

"Like a charm. George's been straight as a string for two years. No nerves or moods until now."

"Any more to the story?"

"That's all there is."

Bradley sighed and slid off the table edge. He smiled at Miss Devon. "If you were in my place, how would you deal with these people?"

"I think your present technique is admirable."

"My technique?" He sounded surprised

"Yes. Sort of cat-and-mouse, isn't it? You apply pressure, then you relax and wait for them to do something. That's what you were doing with Guy, wasn't it? You expected him to make a bolt. That's why you had a man watching him."

"Mercy, I'll have to use some other method with you," he said.

Miss Devon's eyes met his, evenly. "Am I a factor to be dealt with, Inspector?"

He countered. "You're the shrewdest person I've seen tonight. You might be troublesome if things began to point toward you."

"Thank you."

"Plain statement of fact," said Bradley. "Well, I'm going home, get a little rest, and do a lot of thinking. Thanks for the cake."

"I'm glad you liked it."

He started for the hall and then came back to her.

"Will you do me a favor, Miss Devon?"

She looked astonished. "If I can."

"Lock your door when you go to bed tonight!"

"Inspector!"

"I mean it," said Bradley. "I don't trust that active brain of yours not to do considerable guessing. And guessing is going to be an unhealthy pastime around here!"

With that he left.

10

You'd better go to bed, Pat," Miss Devon said.

Pat was still in the corner of the couch. Johnny had risen.

"I … I can't sleep, Aunt Celia. It's almost morning. We'll get some breakfast soon. I want to talk."

"Even if you can't sleep you should rest. In a few hours this mess will really begin."

"It's better to talk to Johnny, Aunt Celia, than just to stew by myself."

"I think," Miss Devon said, "we would be wiser not to stew at all. That's Mr. Bradley's job."

"Aunt Celia! Surely you don't believe …"

"I don't believe that Mr. Bradley is any sort of a fool, Pat. However, you must form your own opinions." She turned and walked down the passage to her room. Johnny settled himself beside Pat. They heard Miss Devon's door close and then a faint click.

Pat looked at Johnny, her eyes widening. "Johnny," she whispered, "Aunt Celia locked her door!"

"So what?"

"Johnny, she's never done that in her life! Ever since we were kids she's left her door unlocked — sometimes open — so we could go to her or she'd hear us if we called."

"Maybe she thinks I might go barging into the wrong room," grinned Johnny. "Don't be jumpy, darling."

Pat held onto his hand. "She's afraid, Johnny. She agrees with Bradley. Oh, Johnny, it's wrong. It has to be wrong! If I believed it … well, I wouldn't want to go on living."

"Hey, you can't start figuring without me, angel. I've got a stake in your future, you know."

"If we could only prove he was wrong," Pat said.

Johnny shook his head. "Inside me, Pat, I'm like you. It's ridiculous. No one had any reason to ... to kill Gloria. But … His voice dropped, doubtfully.

"But what?"

"Well, damn it, Pat, somebody did kill Gloria. He *did* keep her body concealed until tonight. He *did* think up a very clever way to get rid of it. He must have pulled some hocus-pocus with that letter. Why should Gloria leave a flock of blank paper with Linda? No one would open the letter if nothing happened to her!"

"And if someone did switch letters?"

"Well, then you come down to three facts you just can't get around, Pat. The murderer has been at the Garden, at Linda's office, and here. And that last one is the knockout punch, sweet. Almost anyone might fit the first two situations, but there're damn few of us who could have gotten into Gloria's room long enough to make that dummy letter."

"But why, Johnny … *why?"*

Johnny shifted uncomfortably. "You didn't see Guy tonight, or hear what he said."

"Guy was drunk," Pat said. "He wasn't going to be ordered to bed. As soon as you left him, he went out again. Getting away from the man who was following him was probably luck. I'll bet he's at some bar now, really doing a job on himself."

"I wasn't thinking about his skipping."

"What, then?"

"Pat, it'll come out, so you might as well know. Linda and Bradley were there too. First, Guy knew about that letter, and he thought he knew what was in it. As soon as I told him Gloria was dead, he had to get to Linda. He must have been certain the first thing she'd do would be to turn it over to the police. He wanted to stop that."

"But why shouldn't he know what was in it?" Pat objected. "He and Gloria were engaged! Wouldn't she tell him?"

"And wouldn't he go pound the ears off whoever it was she was afraid of? Anyhow, baby, you haven't heard it all. Guy said a lot. A hell of a lot! He told Bradley that when I brought him the news he was relieved. He said he didn't love Gloria and that Gloria didn't love him. He said she was marrying him because she liked yachts!"

"Johnny!"

"He said she had a nasty mind … that she was a bitch! He said their situation had got complicated and that it was easier to go through with it and figure out some kind of a life afterward!"

"Oh, Johnny, he couldn't have!"

"He did. You see now why Bradley had him watched."

"He was drunk!" Pat insisted, with a kind of desperation. "You and I know Guy. He wouldn't kill anyone, Johnny. He's one of the kindest, most generous … Look what he's done for George and for me, for all of us. You mustn't even *think* that he could have …"

"Baby, I can't help thinking," Johnny said. "It's just the way I said. Inside everything revolts against the idea of its being Guy or any of us. But the facts … those damned facts!"

Pat leaned forward, her nose wrinkled in concentration.

"Johnny, if we could prove that it was possible for an outsider to get at Gloria's stationery, wouldn't that punch Mr. Bradley's case full of holes?"

"It wouldn't do it any good."

"Listen. Last weekend Guy took Gloria down to Delaware to some sort of a shooting lodge. Duck hunting."

"Good God! Gloria in a duck blind!"

"Exactly!" said Pat.

"Come again, sweet."

"Gloria wouldn't get herself cold and messy for any ducks. But she went on that weekend all the same. Now what would she do while the others were out? She'd sleep late, maybe have breakfast in bed, and dawdle around till teatime. She might listen to the radio … or read … *or write letters!"*

"Sounds reasonable. But …"

"Johnny, Gloria never wrote letters on anything but her own private letter paper, fastened with those three purple seals. If she knew she was going to have time on her hands, wouldn't she have taken her stationery with her?"

"Pat! By all that's holy! *Did she?"*

"I don't know. Maybe we can find someone to whom she wrote from there. But, Johnny, can Mr. Bradley prove she didn't? And if he can't, wouldn't that show that other people could have stolen some paper? There were forty or fifty people at that lodge."

"Of course they could," Johnny said. "And of those forty or fifty people, friends of Guy's, there must be several who were at the last night of the Horse Show."

"And several who were customers of Linda's."

"Baby, you're a magician. The letter paper is what nailed Bradley's case down! If she had some at that lodge … boy!"

"We can find out from Guy in the morning who was there. Then we can eliminate those who weren't at the Garden and who couldn't have been at Linda's. When Mr. Bradley sees our list …"

"Mr. Bradley is going to be in a hell of a jam."

"You do believe it may be the answer, don't you, Johnny? You do believe that it may be the thing Mr. Bradley missed. That he … *Johnny!"*

Her words had been ended by the sound of a smash on the floor behind them—glass or china. Johnny was on his feet, his fists clenched.

"What the hell!"

Douglas Prayne stood just inside the living-room doorway in the shadows. He was gazing down at a shattered vase.

"Father!"

"I'm sorry I startled you, Patricia," he said. "I … I bumped into that table. I …"

"But, Father, you're still dressed I thought you'd gone to bed."

"Didn't feel like sleep," muttered Prayne. "I … my stomach. I thought perhaps some ginger ale …"

Johnny's fists relaxed. But the kitchen was the other way down the hall.

"Guess I'll forage in the icebox." Prayne's smile was wan. His footsteps were clearly audible now. Johnny and Pat listened, staring at each other. They heard the icebox door open and shut. Then Pat was suddenly clinging to Johnny.

"Don't go away, Johnny!" she pleaded. "I'm scared. Don't leave me!"

11

SOMETIMES I don't understand you," Mr. Julius said. "Act like a man in a trance."

Bradley, draped in his blue dressing gown, broke two eggs into the frying pan on his electric grill. It was nine o'clock in the morning, and a bright winter sun shone through the windows of the kitchenette. Mr. Julius was perched precariously on a kitchen stool, wearing his overcoat, his knitted scarf, and the high-crowned brown derby. He was tapping the receiving end of his seldom-used ear trumpet in the palm of his hand.

"Eating cake with that serpent-tongued female."

"It was an instructive half-hour," said Bradley.

"You're not gathering material for a biography!" snapped Mr. Julius. "You're supposed to be investigating a murder."

Bradley flipped the eggs expertly, poured coffee, removed two slices of toast from the electric toaster, and transferred the eggs to a plate.

"You know George Pelham's story?" he asked as he brought his breakfast to the table.

"Of course."

"What do you think of it?"

"Queer … and tragic. What else?"

"Maybe nothing," said Bradley, buttering his toast.

"Now don't adopt that smug know-it-all attitude! What do you think?"

"I think it's odd," said Bradley, "that two ladies, moving in the same circle, should disappear under almost exactly the same circumstances."

"They never found Dorothy Pelham," Mr. Julius pointed out.

"Perhaps they didn't look in the right place. Sure you won't have some coffee?"

"Positive! And don't ask me again. You're avoiding an issue. What are you going to do now?"

"Nose around," said Bradley cheerfully.

"Great Scott," fumed the old man. "Famous police system! You've done one constructive thing. Had Severied watched. What happened? He made your man look foolish."

Bradley grinned. "Next time you lug bodies around so that the case will come under my jurisdiction, try to arrange to have the friends you want protected a little more willing to help."

"I'm not protecting friends. Pat's the only one I'm concerned about!"

"She's got young Lochinvar."

"What's that?"

"Severied's name for your impetuous young body snatcher."

"Bosh! Young fool! You frighten the pants off the whole crew with a lot of drivel about a clutching hand that's sure to snatch 'em out of their beds. Then you come home and go to sleep

"The mind must have rest and nourishment."

"What about alibis?" Mr. Julius demanded.

"They seemed to be singularly lacking on the three occasions I was interested in. They were all at the Garden; they were all at the dress shop; they all had access to Gloria's room."

"Yes, yes, yes," said Mr. Julius impatiently. "Makes a pretty case. Beautifully indefinite."

"I wonder if you've realized a peculiar fact, Julius?"

"Outside the method of investigation … what?" asked Mr. Julius.

"Do you realize," said Bradley, "that we can only come within a vague few hours of when the murder took place? Sometime between, say, two and ten a.m. Thursday. That we have no idea *where* the murder was committed? That complicates establishing alibis."

"Hmmm," said the old man.

"Suppose I ask one of our suspects where he was between those hours. He says 'Home' … and he can prove it. Maybe that's an alibi and maybe it isn't. Because for all I know that's where the crime was done."

Mr. Julius pondered. "Well," he said, "why not force each other one of 'em to account for his time — each half-hour of his time—from Wednesday night, when Gloria left young Curtin at El Morocco, till one o'clock last night when the body was discovered? I know," he added, "that would be hard, routine work. Boring for an intuitive genius like yourself. But it's common sense."

"Now, now, you're being unusually pettish, any friend. Suppose I got such a time sheet. I'd have to check it. What then? Pelham says, for example, he was with Joe Zilch, an old pal, at a certain time. I go to Joe Zilch … and good old Joe has been tipped off. Everything checks. I can't lock these people up, you know, and keep them from communicating with their friends. There isn't one single direct piece of evidence against anyone but Severied. His knowledge of the letter and then taking a powder might justify my holding him on suspicion.

"All right," said Mr. Julius, "you might have trouble checking.

People aren't inclined to be expansive with detectives. Can't say I blame 'em. But I could check … and Pat and Johnny would help."

"I doubt if you could get an exact enough account from each one of them to make it worthwhile," said Bradley.

"Any objections to my trying? You all laughed at me when I set out to visit every stamp collector in New York to find that kidnapped boy. Well, I found him, didn't I?"

"I haven't any objection," said Bradley. "Might keep you out from underfoot." Then his face grew troubled. "But, for heaven's sake, keep your information to yourself. The minute one of you amateur sleuths gets near the trail, the murderer may slap you down."

"Who, me?"

"Yes, you."

"I've managed to take care of myself for seventy years, without anyone slapping me down."

"It's a miracle," said Bradley, his good humor returning. "Go ahead with your time table. If you find something, I'll be the first to start the applause."

"I doubt it," said the old man sourly.

***

Monahan was sheepish, and being sheepish made him angry. Monahan had trailed some of the wiliest crooks in the country during his career, and to have met his Waterloo at the hands of a drunk with no criminal experience whatsoever was galling. He stood in the foyer of Severied's apartment building, explaining to a faintly smiling Bradley.

"But damn it, Red, I didn't have orders to make an arrest. I was just supposed to tail him. Right from the start he seemed wise to the fact I was there, so I didn't bother to keep out of sight. But he give me the works, all the same."

"How did it happen?"

"He takes a cab from here. It's not ten minutes after that young Curtin dumps him. From what you said I didn't expect no move from him for quite a while. But when he come down in the elevator I bustled out and by luck got myself a cab. Then he starts pullin' the old army game. Round the block … quick spurts uptown and then tryin' to heat me on the lights. Hell, we didn't pay no attention to lights. There wasn't hardly any traffic."

"You hung onto him, eh?"

"Sure. Finally he heads into Fifty-Second Street and stops in front of a dive called the Blue Moon. He pays off his driver and goes in. I hold my own cab, not wantin' to be caught flat-footed, and I follow him in. Well" — and Monahan was growling — "that was that. The place is jammed. I hunt for a while, and then I see he ain't nowhere in sight. I start askin' questions, but no one has noticed him."

"You think the people at the Blue Moon were slipping it to you?" Bradley asked.

"No, I don't, Red. Severied had been in there earlier, makin' trouble. They'd been damn glad to get rid of him. But there's half a dozen fire exits, and you know how dim the lights are in a joint like that. With a crowd millin' around he could've oozed out of one of them without nobody payin' attention." Monahan shrugged. "Bein' alone, I had to take a chance. I ducked out the exit nearest to where he went in, but no soap. Besides, he'd had about ten minutes' start while I was tryin' to locate him inside."

"Well, don't lose sleep over it," Bradley said. "If I'd thought he was likely to play so cagey, I'd have had someone to help you. It's my fault."

"Thanks, Red. You're a good guy to work for. But I promise you if I ever catch up with that ape he won't get away again."

"I'm sure of it. Look here, I want you on this job, Monahan.

Isn't there some place in the building you can knock off a little sleep? If Severied comes back, the elevator boy or the switchboard operator can tip you off."

"I guess I can dig up a place. Incidentally, the night man bunks here in the building. He had a talk with Severied that might interest you. I'd like you to hear it from him anyhow."

A few minutes later a sleepy-eyed Mike was hauled up before the inspector. He wasn't at all averse to finding himself in the limelight. He had seen the morning tabloids before turning in.

"Gee, Inspector, you figure Severied bumped off this gal he was gonna marry?"

"Why should he?"

"She was a swell-lookin' doll," Mike said, "She could've warmed her feet in my bed any time she liked! I wouldn't have done her no harm."

"I can imagine," said Bradley. "Monahan says you had a talk with Severied before he went out."

"Well, you know, just a couple of cracks as I brought him down. I was surprised to see him, on account of when his friend and a taxi driver brought him in his legs would hardly hold him up. Ten minutes after the friend leaves he's as spry as a chicken. Well maybe not that spry. He was a little shaky, but he knew what he was doin' all right."

"The conversation," Bradley prompted.

"Oh, yeah. Well, lately he's been goin' out early in the morning … that is, when he stayed here in town which wasn't often. Duck huntin'. He was crazy about it. I figured, drunk as he was, he was headin' for the country. 'Goin' huntin'? I ask him. 'Yes,' he says. 'Ducks?' I ask him. 'No,' he says. He gives me a funny look. 'I'm goin' man huntin',' he says. 'You ought to try it,' he says. 'It's so unpredictable!' he says. Well, cripes, Inspector. I figured he was real soused alter all."

"It could be," Bradley murmured. "So he was going man

hunting!" He shook his head sadly.

"Maybe he had a hunch who done in his girl," Monahan suggested. "If somebody knocked off my old lady and I thought I knew who, I'd be kind of likely to settle accounts myself."

"From the way Severied talked about his intended bride," said Bradley, "I think he'd be more likely to pin a decoration on the guy." He belted up his trench coat. "I've a man out at his Long Island place, and I'm having his boat watched. I guess it's the best we can do. Monahan, you arrange to stay here. If Severied shows, sit on him."

"It'll be a pleasure," said Monahan.

Bradley started to turn away, and then be asked Mike another question. "Does Severied have a regular cleaning woman?"

"No, sir. You see, he doesn't use this apartment regular. I mean he don't really *live* here. This time of year, when there's late parties in town, he's around more often. Pretty soon he'll be goin' South and we won't see him at all."

"What about the cleaning?"

"Oh, the superintendent's wife does for him, Inspector. But she don't go up unless Mr. Severied sends for her special."

"She live here in the building?"

"Sure."

"Call her on the house phone and ask her when she last cleaned the apartment."

"Okay." Mike went to the switchboard.

"What's the angle, Red?" Monahan asked.

Bradley rubbed the end of his chin. "Here's the way it is," he said. "The murderer must have kept Gloria Prayne's body for at least two days in a place where no one would barge in and find it. Now an apartment … with no cleaning woman or maid to worry about …"

"I get it," said Monahan. He looked eagerly at Mike, who was returning.

"Mrs. Rasmussen says she ain't been up there in over a week," he reported.

"That does it!" declared Monahan. "The sneaking tramp killed his own girl, kept the body hid up there till he could get rid of it, and then took it on the lam. Fooled you by playin' drunk. It's clear as the nose on your face."

"Umm," said Bradley. "That's what I don't like about it, Monahan. Why would a man who's been so damned slick up to now blow the whole game by running out?"

Bradley had just stepped from his taxi onto the pavement in front of the building on Ninety-first Street when he was surrounded by a horde of noisy reporters.

"Where the hell have you been, Inspector?"

Bradley smiled. "Waiting for the dough to rise," he said.

"Okay, pal, give!"

"Let's see," said Bradley, jingling the change in his pocket. "Miss Gloria Prayne, daughter of Mr. Douglas Prayne of East Ninety-First Street, was found strangled to death in the back of her own automobile at one o'clock Sunday morning. The car was parked outside Madison Square Garden. The gruesome discovery was made by Mr. John Curtin, friend of the family, who at once — or almost at once — notified the police. Inspector Bradley of the Homicide Division promises an early arrest."

One of the reporters groaned. "He's in a light mood!"

"You can't get away with that, Red. Give us the low-down."

Bradley began the ritual of loading his pipe from the red tin. "Taxpayers indignant," he said. "Police make no progress in Prayne case. Urge liquidation of detective in charge. That do, boys?"

"Red, for God's sake, we mean business. Nobody in this place will give us anything. We've tried to get a statement from Guy Severied, but we can't locate him."

"If you do," said Bradley, "let me know!"

"You mean you don't know where he is?"

"I mean I don't know where he is … and I'd like to," said Bradley.

"Oh, boy! Has he skipped out on you, Red?"

Bradley shrugged. "Dunno, boys. I just haven't been able to locate him either."

"Maybe he hasn't heard the news! Maybe he's off in the country somewhere!"

"Maybe," said Bradley. He wasn't giving.

"But you got any leads, Red, any clues?"

Bradley hesitated. "Yes, I've got a clue," he said.

They crowded around him, pencils poised. "Let's have it!"

"The murderer was at Madison Square Garden last night," said Bradley, "along with about twenty thousand other people. By a process of elimination we should be able, in six or eight months, to — "

"You bastard, Bradley!"

Bradley went serious. "Sorry, boys, there isn't a thing. Not for the general public. I'll tell you this much. I've held conversation with the murderer since last night."

"Then you know who it is?"

"I'd be lying in my teeth if I said so. I've talked to quite a lot of people. He was among them. And one of these days I'm liable to put' the finger on him. Well, so long. There ought to be enough dope in your society editor's files to keep you going."

***

Bradley did not go in the Madison Avenue entrance. Instead, he walked around the corner to the arched doors of the Crop and Spur. Cut in one of these was a smaller door just about large enough for a person of Bradley's size. It wasn't locked, and he let himself into the high-ceilinged tanbark ring.

As he drew the door to behind him, a rider on a black horse swept past, throwing up dirt and grit on his overcoat. Bradley kept to the wall and made his way to a raised platform, railed in, on which were set several wicker chairs. Bradley sat down in one of them with a sigh of contentment, pushed his hat to the back of his red head, and stretched out his feet. Smoke billowed from his pipe.

The rider on the black horse was George Pelham. Nothing about the captain's horsemanship suggested that his nerves were worn to the raw by last night's tragedy. There were six or eight jumps around the ring — brush, an in-and-out on the far side, a murderous-looking triple bar, a stone wall, and a number of simple double bars.

The horse Pelham rode was a handful. Just as Bradley settled in his chair the black refused, swerving dizzily outside the wings of the triple bar. Pelham might have been part of the animal. He reined the horse in, patted his neck, spoke to him in a low, gentle voice. Then he walked him up to the jump. The horse eyed it suspiciously, ears cocked.

Pelham took him back a way and started him for it once more. Again in front of the bars the horse stopped dead, as if operated by an invisible air brake. Pelham bent forward, stroked his neck, and continued to talk.

He wheeled and rode off, apparently giving up the idea of the triple bar. They went over two of the easy jumps.

The black was a tremendously powerful jumper, taking off a good distance from the obstacle and literally hurtling through the air. Without slacking his pace Pelham headed a third time for the triple bar. There was no spur or whip applied as they approached; but Bradley could hear the captain's voice, encouraging, urging. For a moment it looked as though the horse would still refuse. His rush slowed … he almost balked. And then Pelham seemed, with his hands, to lift the horse clear over the jump.

"Something I can do for you, sir?" asked a voice at Bradley's elbow.

The inspector turned to confront a small, gray-haired man with a leathery, wind-tanned face. He wore riding breeches, canvas puttees, and a dark-blue turtle-necked sweater. He held a cap in his hand.

"No, thanks," said Bradley. "Just looking around. Captain Pelham certainly knows his stuff."

"He does that," said the man. "He's patience and gentleness to the tip of his small finger, sir. You'll never see him frighten a horse into taking a hurdle. When he's through with that green devil, a child'll be able to ride him."

"I can well believe it."

"I'm sorry, sir, but the school is closed today," the man went on. "We've had bad trouble here, sir."

"I know. I'm Inspector Bradley. You're Peter Shea?"

"That's right, sir."

"Sit down, Shea. Like to talk to you."

"Yes, sir," the groom said, but he remained standing.

"Shea, is there a way up to the Prayne's apartment without going around to the front entrance?"

"Oh, yes sir. There's a back stair. But it doesn't go to any of the tenants' living quarters.. You see, this was an old loft building which Miss Pat and the Captain leased. When Mr. Severied remodeled it into apartments, he built the back stair special, just to go to Miss Pat's."

"I see. If Miss Pat sent you for something, you'd use that stair?"

"Yes, sir. I do that, often."

"Then any of the pupils or customers or whatever you call them here at the school could get into the apartment that way?"

"Well, sir, they could if there was someone to let them in."

"The door into the apartment is kept locked?"

"Oh, yes, sir,"

"Then you have a key?"

"No, sir … not exactly. There is a key, kept hid in a special place. Only the Captain, myself, and the family know where it is."

"A stranger, who wanted to get into the apartment, couldn't just slip up those back stairs when you weren't looking?"

"Not unless he knew where the key was."

Bradley sucked on his pipe. "Bad business this, Shea."

The groom's lips tightened. "It is that, sir. I … well, Miss Gloria didn't have any truck with the school, but I know what it means to Miss Pat and the Captain."

"Pretty cut up, are they?"

"Naturally, sir. Wouldn't you be, if your own sister …"

"Of course, Shea. Tell me about the school. How is it run?"

"Well, sir, it is just that, strictly speaking, a school. We don't rent out horses for riding in the park. We teach people to jump. It depends how green you are how long you need. If you don't know anything at all about jumping, we take you through a series of twenty-four lessons."

"I see."

"The idea is we put you on the gentlest horse we've got, first. That's Baldy, horse number one. You go on from, that to horse number two and so on. When you've ridden the twenty-fourth horse, sir, you know all the answers."

Bradley watched Pelham dismount and lead the black down the basement ramp.

"Mercy," he said. "I hope I don't have to go through as tough a schedule as that to learn all the answers in this case."

"I hope not, sir," Shea said politely.

Just then the little door in the big door opened, and Bradley saw Miss Celia Devon squeeze her way through. She was loaded down with bundles. He went across the tanbark to greet her.

"Can I help you?" he asked.

"If you start unloading me, I'll fall apart," she said. "Murder or no murder, my family has to eat. Incidentally, I locked my door, Inspector, and I don't think anyone tried to batter it down."

"I didn't think they really would … last night," said Bradley. "And how is your family?"

"Pat was asleep when I went out. She and Johnny were buzzing till breakfast; and then that young man hustled off, full of mystery. If you're not careful, Inspector, those two will beat you to a solution."

"Keep your fingers crossed on that," Bradley said.

"Inspector, I do believe you're an alarmist. I've half persuaded myself, in spite of your beautiful reasoning, that Gloria was killed by a night-club gangster."

"Fine," said Bradley. "Keep saying that out loud to anyone who asks you. You'll be safer. How's Mr. Prayne bearing up?"

"Douglas trotted off to see his lawyer at the crack of dawn. He wants to be certain no one infringes on his rights. Poor Douglas, this has been a terrible blow to him — losing one of the richest men in America for a son-in-law."

In the basement stable Peter Shea hurried up to where Pelham had crosstied the black and was removing the saddle.

"I'll take over, sir," he said.

"Thanks," Pelham said. He took a cigarette from his pocket and lit it, but he did not go away. He watched Shea going over the black's sleek coat with a cloth. The groom whistled softly between his, teeth as he worked. Presently he became aware of Pelham's somber eyes fixed on him.

"He's coming along fine, sir," Shea said, patting the horse's flank. "In another week or two we should be able to put him into service."

Pelham nodded. "He's got a baby mouth. Goes crazy if you aren't light as a feather."

Shea took a damp sponge and swabbed the black's lips with it. "He's got grand power when he takes off, sir. Looks like he was going clean over the rafters."

Pelham flicked the ash from his cigarette. "Wasn't that Inspector Bradley you were talking to?"

"Yes, sir."

"What did he want?"

"Nothing much, Captain. Asked if anyone could get into the Praynes' apartment the back way if they didn't have a key. I explained how it was. Then he got chatting about what a lovely way you have with a horse, sir, and asked me about how we run the school and all."

"Nothing else?"

"No, sir."

"You *haven't* seen any strangers using the back stair, have you, Peter?"

"No, sir."

"Or anyone outside the family … like Mr. Severied or Miss Linda or Mr. Curtin?"

"No, sir. Leastways, not without you or Miss Pat with them." The groom looked at Pelham's anxious face. "Captain, if there's anything I can do to help …"

'There's nothing, Peter. We've just got to sit tight while Bradley tries to pin murder on one of us! We've got to go on with our business … if there's any left after this scandal! Polishing bits and soaping tack … while Bradley decides on a victim."

"Is it true, sir, that Mr. Severied has … well, not shown up?"

Pelham's eyes flashed. "You know as well as I do, Peter, that Guy never had anything to do with murder."

"Of course, sir, but it is funny he should …"

"I'm afraid he's in some sort of a jam," Pelham said. He lifted a hand to cover his tired eyes for an instant. "If we only knew where to find him, we might be able to help."

***

Just as Bradley emerged onto the sidewalk, Rube Snyder hopped out of a police car and came up to him.

"Here's what you wanted, Red," he said. "A warrant to search Severied's apartment."

"Swell. Let's go have a look now," said Bradley.

Rube drove the car back downtown. "What do you expect to find in this bird's place, Red?" he asked.

Bradley smiled. "I'm darned if I know, Rube. We've got to do something active to keep the commissioner satisfied."

"Don't talk like a dope," said Rube. "You never do nothin' without a reason."

"Maybe I was ashamed to tell you what I expect to find," said Bradley.

"What, Red?"

"Nothing," said Bradley unhappily.

"Come off it, Red!"

"It's true, Rube. The place where Gloria Prayne's body was hidden is probably the place where the murder was committed. So far Severied's is the only apartment I've heard of where it would be safe to hide a body."

"But, hell, Red, that sounds reasonable. Why don't you expect to find nothin'?"

"Because." Bradley said, "I don't think the body was hidden there."

Rube was still looking puzzled when he parked the sedan on Sixty-third Street. There was no sign of Monahan, and the switchboard operator told them that Severied hadn't returned and that the detective was asleep in the porter's room in the basement. Bradley explained about his warrant, and the superintendent was sent for to bring his pass key.

A few minutes later the two men from headquarters and Mr. Rasmussen, a grizzled Dane who smoked a monstrous curve-stemmed pipe, went up in the elevator.

They got out at Severied's floor and walked along the tiled hallway. Just as they were opposite the apartment door, it was flung open. A man came out, head lowered, running like a halfback in a clear field.

He charged straight into Bradley and was brought up short by the inspector, who had braced himself for the onslaught. It was Johnny Curtin.

Johnny tried to wrench free, looked up, and saw who it was that held him.

"Inspector, thank God it's you!" he cried in a hoarse voice. He gestured wildly toward the open door of the apartment. "Guy! They got him! He's dead. Oh, my God, the whole back of his head is blown off."

Bradley and Rube moved quickly. The inspector was the first through the door; but he stopped as he crossed the threshold, and his teeth clamped down hard on the stem of his pipe.

The dead man, sprawled on the rug, still wore his overcoat, although his brown felt hat had rolled a few feet away. The back of his head was not pretty. Some sort of high caliber bullet had obliterated its shape.

Bradley's face had gone white and set. "How the devil did he get up here? Is everybody permanently asleep at the switch?" He stepped into the room; halted once more, taking a side view. "Good Lord!" he said. He knelt down, without touching the body, and peered at the face buried in the thick nap of the rug. "This isn't Severied!" he said.

"Not Guy!" Johnny choked. "Then who in God's name …"

Bradley stood up, dusting off his hands. "It's Douglas Prayne," he said.

12

"MR. PRAYNE!" Johnny started into the foyer.

"Hold it!" Rube Snyder collared Johnny and yanked him hack into the hall. There was no sound as Bradley stood in the doorway, staring stonily around. Then Rasmussen, the superintendent, began to whimper like a frightened child.

"Cheesusgott! Cheesusgott!" he said, over and over again. "They murdert him!"

There was no gun visible and, unless Prayne's body had fallen on the weapon, it was gone. Bradley was not yet prepared to search for it. He disappeared through the living room into the back of the apartment. He was away only a moment.

"No one here," he said. He walked out into the hall, pulled the door closed, and the lock snapped. "The key," he said to Rasmussen.

The superintendent produced a ring of keys that jingled like sleigh bells in his fingers.

"Which one is it?"

Rasmussen pointed, and Bradley slipped the proper key off the ring and pocketed it.

"Inspector!" Johnny broke out. "Let me explain about this. I—"

"Shut up, you!" Rube growled. His fingers were still hooked into Johnny's collar. Johnny tried to shake himself free. "Now, now, baby, don't get rough!"

"Let him go," said Bradley.

"Okay," muttered Rube, disappointed.

"Rasmussen," Bradley said, "rout out Monahan, my man who's sleeping in your porter's room."

"Ja … ja."

"And have your employees stand by for questioning. If any one of them leaves the building, I'll lock 'em up for life."

"Ja. I tell dem." He scurried for the elevator, still mumbling under his breath, "Cheesusgott!"

"Rube! Go downstairs to the switchboard. Call headquarters and get the squad here at once — the M.E., fingerprint man, photographer … the works."

"Okay, Red."

"And get the nearest radio car to us pronto."

"Right!" And Rube was off.

Bradley ignored Johnny, his frosty eyes fixed on some distant point in space. Johnny nervously waited. At last the gray eyes came to rest on him.

"Well?" said Bradley.

Words poured out of Johnny. "Inspector. I'd only gotten here about two minutes before you. Pat and I had a theory about Gloria's murder, and we thought Guy could help us. He has a privately listed phone and neither Pat nor I knew the number, so I came instead of calling. I rang the doorbell, and there wasn't any answer. When I started to knock, I saw the door wasn't latched, so I pushed it open and went in. I … I saw him lying there and … and I didn't look closely. I … I took it for granted it was Guy and ran for help … and there you were. I … I … that's all I know."

Bradley just looked at him.

"You've got to believe me," Johnny said. "That's exactly

what happened."

"Didn't you announce yourself?" Bradley asked.

"No. I … well, I thought you might be having the place watched."

"And you didn't want me to know about this visit!" Bradley finished for him. "What made you think you'd find Severied here?"

"Pat and I figured Guy was simply being cantankerous when he walked out. A souse is stubborn, Inspector. We thought he'd come back home to get some sleep, after he'd had his way."

"Mercy," said Bradley coldly. "Practical psychologists! You didn't see anyone come out of this apartment? No one passed you in the hall or was waiting for the elevator?"

"Not a soul. No one, Inspector."

"Did you touch anything in that room?"

"Good God, no. I … I took one look and ran!"

"The doorknob?"

"I … I'm not sure. I think I just pushed the door open. I did ring the bell, though."

"That will be a help! You see Douglas Prayne this morning?"

"You mean at home?"

"Where the devil do you think I mean? You spent the night at his apartment."

"I did, Bradley. But that's no reason for you to …"

"Answer my question!"

"Yes … yes, I saw him. But he left before I did."

"How long ago was that?"

"Why … why, it can't be much more than two hours."

Bradley groaned. "And where did he say he was going?"

"To his lawyer's. He wanted advice on how to deal with … with you, Inspector!"

"Did he mention Severied … or that he was coming here?"

"Not in front of me, Inspector."

"And you remained at the Praynes' for another hour and a half?"

"Yes, sir. Pat and I had breakfast … and talked some more. You see, we have a theory that—"

"I don't give a good God damn about your theories, Curtin. Then you came straight here?"

"In a cab."

The elevator gate opened and Rube, with Monahan in tow, joined them. Monahan looked scared.

"Inspector, I swear I …"

"Stop worrying," Bradley said. "Unless Severied himself got by you you're in the clear."

"Thanks, Inspector. What do you want me to do now?"

"Work over the elevator man, the switchboard operator, and the night man. Someone besides Prayne came up and into this apartment. Find out who it was or get a description. One of 'em must have seen Prayne; Find out exactly what time he got here. Find out who left after that and when."

"The night man wasn't on duty. Inspector. He …"

"We don't know when the murderer arrived," Bradley said. "He may have come earlier and waited. Sweat it all out of 'em, Monahan. Get tough if you have to."

"Count on me, Inspector."

Bradley turned to Rube. "Take Mr. Curtin downstairs. When the radio car comes, have 'em take him down to headquarters and lock him up!"

"Inspector!" Johnny cried. "I've got to get back to Pat. I—"

"Take him away," Bradley said.

"You can't do this, Bradley! What's the charge against me?"

"You find too many dead bodies, Curtin," Bradley said. "Have him booked as a material witness, Rube."

"Come on, sweetie pie," said Rube.

"After that, Rube, round up the rest of 'em and bring 'em downtown. Miss Prayne. Miss Devon, Miss Marsh, Pelham ... the whole kit and caboodle."

"How about a general alarm for Severied?"

"No," said Bradley.

"Hell, Red, you want to find him, don't you?"

"No!"

Rube was bewildered. "But, Red ... nobody busted this door! Severied himself must of come back ..."

"Will you get moving?" Bradley demanded.

"Okay, Red, it's your case. I guess you know what you're doin'."

"Thanks," said Bradley, "for the compliment."

The squad from headquarters descended on Guy Severied's flat and gave it the works. Douglas Prayne's body was photographed from every conceivable angle. Its outline was drawn in chalk on the rug. The medical examiner gave it his attention before the stretcher bearers carried it downstairs to the morgue wagon. There was no gun lying beneath the body.

The M. E. announced that Prayne had been dead probably not more than two hours and not less than one.

"Find out what time he ate breakfast, and I can give it to you on the nail after the autopsy," he advised Bradley.

The fingerprint man went over the apartment inch by inch, dusting, photographing. When he was through, he had a fine collection of matching items that were unquestionably Guy's. There were others not readily identified. Prayne had left none, since he had been wearing gloves.

In the end Bradley gave the place a personal going over. Certain facts emerged.

Either the murderer had had a key to the apartment or Severied had not shut the door securely when he went out the night before. This latter possibility appeared less probable, since the lock was of the snap variety and there was nothing in the foyer to keep the door from swinging to.

Douglas Prayne had been wearing rubbers. He had tracked in moisture and mud from the street. The result was a clear enough trail on Guy's rug. Prayne had come into the apartment, crossed to the chair by the fireplace and sat there for some time, to judge by the fuzz he had kicked up on the nap of the rug. Then, apparently, he had started to leave. The return trail led almost to the foyer. There it stopped … because there Payne had been shot in the hack of the head. There were no other distinguishable marks on the rug; but it seemed fairly clear that Prayne had sat talking to someone, and that the someone had shot him as he was leaving.

Bradley had just finished noting these facts when Monahan reported.

"Nothing that's gonna help, Inspector," he said ruefully. "But I'll have another crack at it. There's just one thing they all swear to. Severied didn't come back. At least no one saw him, it would have been possible, of course, for him to have waited until the elevator man was at one of the upper floors, and then to have sneaked up the fire stairs. But that could only have happened during the night man's shift, when there's no one at the switchboard."

"But you were on watch all during that shift," said Bradley.

"And I never left that hallway, not even to go to the toilet," Monahan insisted. "But there was a time he could have come back, Inspector. After he gave me the slip at the Blue Moon. See what I mean? I spent maybe three quarters of an hour lookin' and callin' you and gettin' back here. If he came straight here, he might've made it."

"Right." agreed Bradley. "It's a chance. But how did he get out again? To have killed Prayne he'd have to have left some time in the last hour. He couldn't have used the fire stairs then without being seen, could he?"

"Positively not. And he didn't use the elevator. Unless he pulled a human-fly act, he just couldn't have got out."

"How about Prayne? Did they see him come in?"

Monahan's round face was somber. "Here's the trouble, Inspector. There's three apartments on this floor besides Severied's. One of them is occupied by a fellow named Guilfoyle. You've heard of him? He does a Broadway column for one of the tabloids. All kinds of people come to see him at all hours of the day and night. The elevator boys have got so used to a procession goin' up to this Guilfoyle's they just don't pay much attention to anyone for or from this floor."

"That's just dandy," said Bradley. "A tabloid columnist! How come he isn't in our hair already?"

"He went out about half an hour before you came, Inspector. Now get this. The day man remembers — he *thinks* — bringin' Prayne up about nine o'clock, That'd be about an hour and three quarters before he was found. As for anyone else … well, he says Guilfoyle's already had at least half a dozen visitors this morning. I mean at the time he figured they were Guilfoyle's friends. He doesn't remember much about them except he says a couple of 'em were dames."

"Can he describe them?"

Monahan was disgusted. "I tried that. Two arms, two legs … you know, the usual useless stuff. He did say one of 'em was no chicken. Gray hair."

Bradley's eyes narrowed. After a moment he dropped his hand on Monahan's shoulder. "Couple of tough breaks for you," he said. "But you've done your best. Stick here until I send someone. If anyone asks for Severied, hang onto 'em. When your relief shows, bring this elevator boy down to headquarters. I want him to look over some people. Maybe he'll recognize somebody."

Back in his office Bradley dictated his own reports. Then as Rube had not yet arrived with his roundup of suspects, he had Johnny Curtin brought in.

Johnny was tight-lipped and truculent when a uniformed policeman left him standing in front of Bradley's desk.

"I came to you last night because you were Mr. Julius' friend," he said, before Bradley could speak. "He was sure of your help and consideration. Now you're kicking us around just the way we could expect to be treated by any dumb mick on the force."

"Sit down." said Bradley, his voice deceptively mild.

"I'll stand," Johnny said.

Bradley took his pipe from his pocket and began to fill it from a stone crock on his desk. His deliberateness was a sign that he was fighting for control of his own temper.

"You know, Curtin," he said, "you are not up before the headmaster at prep school for having put a snake in the Latin teacher's bed! Two people have been murdered. We don't kid about killings down here." He held a match to his pipe. "I tried to be considerate last night. What's the result? If I'd locked every damned one of you up on suspicion, Douglas Prayne wouldn't be having his guts cut open by the medical examiner at this moment."

Johnny moistened his lips. "I *do* appreciate your position. But people's nerves can't stand this sort of thing, Bradley. Not ordinary people. I … I … Cripes, I can't get the picture of Prayne out of my head."

"Got any idea why Prayne went to Guy's?" Bradley asked.

"No. It was the truth, Bradley, when I said he never mentioned it."

"Were he and Severied friendly?"

"I don't know. I didn't often see them together. They acted just like you'd expect a man and his prospective son-in-law to act."

"Then you wouldn't expect Prayne to pour out his troubles to Severied?"

"Well, in this case ... I mean it doesn't seem unnatural."

"Perhaps not. Let's get down to you. You and Pat have a theory about Gloria's murder. How does it stand up now Mr. Prayne is dead?"

"I don't know. I ... I haven't been able to think very clearly. But it doesn't change the basic possibilities. We still could be right."

"I've got time to listen to it now," said Bradley.

Johnny told him about Pat's suggestion that Gloria had taken her writing materials with her to the shooting lodge in Delaware. "We thought if we could get a list of the people at the lodge and then whittle it down by checking with those who were at the Garden and at Linda's we'd be able to show you how some outsider could be involved. It's not such a dumb idea, is it?"

Bradley smoked in silence, "No, because it could have happened," he said finally. "But I don't think it did. For several reasons. There was nothing chancy about Gloria's murder, Curtin. It was carefully thought out and executed. The murderer couldn't count on Gloria's taking those writing materials with her anywhere. He, had to get 'em from where he knew they were, in Gloria's room."

"But ..."

"There's an outside chance you're right," Bradley went on, "if Severied is our man. He might know in advance that Gloria would have with her what he wanted."

"You suspect Guy?"

"Not talking," he said, and smiled. "So you went to Severied's apartment this morning to get a list of the people who were on that shooting party last week end?"

"That's gospel, Inspector."

"My guess is that you're just plain lucky, Curtin. If you'd

turned up a bit sooner, we'd have had two corpses instead of one; and I think that's gospel!"

The phone rang. It was Rube.

"I got the three, from uptown, Red," he said. "I'm at Miss Marsh's shop now, but she don't want to come. She wants to talk to you."

"Put her on."

"Inspector Bradley? Your sergeant has just told me the terrible news!"

"It's not nice," said Bradley.

"He says I'm to come to headquarters with him, Mr. Bradley. I want to help, but my foreign buyer is sailing tomorrow. It's absolutely necessary that I have this day clear. If I knew anything, it would be different. But I haven't seen or talked with any of the Praynes since last night. Perhaps I could rush things, and late this afternoon — "

"Put Snyder on the wire, Miss Marsh," said Bradley pleasantly.

"Hello, Red. Okay for her to stay here?"

"Bring her down," said Bradley, *"now!"* He put the receiver back in place and looked up at Johnny. "Did you know Dorothy Pelham?" he asked.

Johnny frowned. "No. Pat's told me about her, of course. I never knew her."

"All right, Curtin, that's' all for now. I'm keeping you here, however."

"But, Inspector, Pat — "

"Will be here in about twenty minutes. Keep your shirt on, Curtin. I won't bite her!"

***

Bradley was alone for only a moment. The door opened and a man in a sloppy suit came in. He was carrying a small piece of

Kleenex in his hand, which he put down on Bradley's desk and unfolded. In it was a small piece of metal, flattened out on one side.

"You've got a report for me on the bullet so soon, Erhardt?" said Bradley.

Erhardt shook his head. "I haven't made tests yet. Without the gun I can't do much. This is a .45 caliber slug … they tear quite a hole."

"I noticed," Bradley said.

"Anybody in this case with army connections … maybe during the last war?"

"So that's how it is!" said Bradley softly.

"A guess, Inspector ... but p'raps it will stand up. I figure this bullet was fired from a type of automatic issued to officers early in the World War. There are a lot of them still floating around. If you've any soldiers mixed up in your case …"

"We've got a ducky ex-service man, Erhardt, with a bad case of nerves and a life with too damned many coincidences."

Erhardt grinned. "Then keep your eye on him."

13

SHE's pretty sore," Rube said. His shoulders were hunched and his face was red. "She's goin' to complain to the commissioner, the mayor, the governor, and maybe the White House."

Bradley chuckled. "I had an idea she might not be pleased."

"She had this buyer dame callin' her lawyer when we left the shop," Rube said.

"Mercy, lawyers are popular this morning. Prayne was supposed to be hunting his too. Well, fortunately we don't need a grand-jury indictment to hold people for questioning."

"You gettin' anywhere, Red?"

"I'm lousy with information," Bradley said. "I've got a job for you." He picked up a document from his desk. "Search warrant for the apartment of Captain George Pelham. Get up there."

"What am I looking for?"

"A gun," said Bradley. "Make it snappy, because I don't want to talk to him till I know whether he's got one and what kind it is."

"I'm on my way," Rube said.

"Just a minute, Rube. How did the rest of them take the news?"

"Kind of dazed … that is, the Prayne girl and this Pelham. They both acted like I'd poleaxed 'em. The old girl is somethin' different again. I wouldn't like to play no poker with her, Red. That pan of hers don't tell you nothin'!"

"Interesting type, Miss Devon. Okay, on your horse. Phone me the minute you've covered the place."

"You think I'll be likely to find this rod?"

"I'll be dumfounded if you do," said Bradley. "I just want to know that it *isn't* there."

"You figure he got rid of it after he shot Prayne?"

"Who got rid of it?"

"Why, Pelham of course. Isn't that the way it lines up?"

"Somebody could have borrowed it," said Bradley.

Rube looked aggrieved. "Too many people snoop around in too many places in this case to suit me."

"Ain't it the truth!" said Bradley. "Roll, my friend!"

***

"Miss Prayne," said Bradley into the communicator. Then he poured himself a drink at the water cooler in the corner, dropped the paper cup in a wire trash basket, and walked past the green steel filing cabinets to the door. He was there when the uniformed cop brought Pat in.

Rube's description had been accurate. Pat moved like a sleepwalker.

Bradley took her arm and led her to the plain oak chair beside his desk.

"I'm sorry, Miss Prayne," he said gently. "I ought to have been able to save you this."

She avoided his look of sympathy. "Don't be nice to me, Mr. Bradley," she said. "Just ask your questions without thinking about my feelings. It'll be easier that way. Please."

"Right. We've got a fight on our hands with a very tough guy. I wasn't wrong last night when I said there is danger. And it's not over yet."

She stared past him at the crook-necked desk lamp with a green and white shade.

"I'm not going to ask you much about your father," Bradley said. "As I understand it, you sat up all night with young Curtin talking over a theory designed to upset my chain of reasoning."

She nodded.

"You had breakfast. After that your father went out, saying he was going to see his lawyer. That correct?"

"Yes. That must have been about a quarter to nine."

"Curtin stayed on with you, and then went off to see Severied?"

"He stayed quite a long time, Inspector. More than an hour. We thought Guy would need plenty of sleep after the night before."

"I see. Your father didn't mention going to Severied's himself?"

"No. He just spoke of his lawyer, Mr. Partridge. He thought we all needed advice."

Bradley rocked back and forth in his swivel chair, the tips of his fingers pressed together. "Have you any idea why your father wanted to see Severied?"

Pat's eyes fastened on her strong brown hands clasped in her lap. "I've thought about it, Inspector. I … I guess I haven't thought about much else since Sergeant Snyder brought us the news. There's one thing … but it's probably crazy."

"Let's hear it."

"Long after Father and Aunt Celia had gone to bed, Johnny and I were still planning to prove to you that the murderer could have gotten the letter paper somewhere else besides our apartment. We decided to ask Guy for a list of people who had been in Delaware. And right in the middle of it someone knocked a vase off a table by the door. We were both startled. It was father. He said he hadn't been able to sleep. He hadn't undressed. I … I couldn't help thinking that he'd been listening."

"So?"

"Father was upset by what you said about our all being in danger," Pat said. "I … I think he didn't want Johnny and me to go on with the investigation, but he knew it wouldn't do any good to argue with us. Perhaps he went to Guy's to get him to persuade us not to meddle."

"I see. Then you think …"

"I think the murderer was waiting for Guy at his apartment. When Father got there, well, the murderer had to shoot him in … in self-defense."

Bradley's eyebrows went up. "So you don't think Severied killed your father?"

"I know he didn't!"

"Because?"

"Because I know Guy!"

"You're a great girl," Bradley said. "I wish you were my friend. Tell me about Dorothy Pelham."

For the first time Pat looked straight at him, and there was no doubting her astonishment.

"I know the general story of her disappearance," said Bradley. "But I'm curious. What was she like?"

"But, Inspector, what's that to do with what's happened now?"

"It's just a hunch of mine. May give me a line on how to deal with Pelham."

"When Dorothy disappeared," Pat said, "I was fifteen. I thought she was marvelous. I wanted to be like her, to look like her, to talk like her."

"Mercy! So she was that attractive?"

"She was." Enthusiasm sounded in Pat's voice. "Do you remember Ruth Chatterton in the movies a long time ago?"

"Very well."

"Dorothy was like that, only she seemed younger. She talked with a slight British accent, and I used to imitate her. On a horse she was like Diana. That was what got me working with horses. I knew I could never really look like Dorothy, or act like her, but I could learn to ride as well as she did."

"Were she and Pelham happy?"

"I never saw two people so happy," Pat said. "They had the same tastes, and they both did everything so well. George was different then. Gay, witty, always joking and laughing. And he looked years younger than he does now. If you'd known Dorothy, you'd understand what losing her could mean to him."

"Wasn't there ever any guessing as to what happened to her?"

"A great deal, Mr. Bradley. But we all came to believe that she met with some sort of accident and couldn't be identified."

"But they must have canvassed hospitals and that sort of thing?"

"I guess they did," said Pat. "I was too young to be much help. And I was too broken-hearted to pay attention to what people did. But I know that the police, and private detectives, and George and Guy did everything that could be done."

"And that's all that anyone knows about it?"

"Yes."

"Did your sister Gloria ever talk about it to you … recently?"

Pat frowned. "Why … perhaps," she said. "We still do talk about it occasionally. When something about George comes up. I mean how he's changed, and doesn't get any fun out of anything. Gloria may have said something like, 'If Dorothy were here

George wouldn't do so-and-so.' But if you mean really discuss the case, she didn't."

Bradley sat forward, and the spring on the swivel chair creaked. Miss Prayne, that's all I'm going to bother you with now ... except to ask you please not to play detective! Your Uncle Julius is trying to tabulate a set of alibis. You can help him with that, and it may go to prove your theory about an outsider. But don't start investigating on your own."

She looked at him steadily. Then: "I guess we've got to trust you, Mr. Bradley," she said.

"Good girl. You'll find Curtin in one of the waiting rooms. But you'll have to stay here for a while until I'm sure I don't need you."

***

Monahan came in then.

"Everything quiet up the line," he told Bradley. "No one's been to see Severied, and he hasn't turned up himself. I brought the elevator boy with me like you said."

"Good. We can let him give this gang the once over and then send him back to his job." Bradley pressed a buzzer.

"Get all those people here for questioning into the main waiting room," Bradley ordered the policeman who answered. "Have a couple of stenographers put on their hats and coats and mingle; also one or two plain-clothesmen and any policewoman you can find on duty. I want about a dozen people in there."

"Okay, Inspector."

"Bring the boy in, Monahan."

The day elevator boy was not as confident a specimen as Mike. He was frightened, and kept blotting at his face handkerchief.

"Take it easy, son," Bradley said. "There's nothing very tough about this. In a couple of minutes you're going into the waiting room and sit down. There'll be a dozen or so Take your time and look 'em over carefully. Then come out and report to me whether you recognize any of 'em as having been at your building."

"Gee, Inspector, I hate to put the finger on anyone," the boy said.

Bradley consoled him. "There may be someone there who called on Guilfoyle. They wouldn't have anything to do with the murder. You'll be saving us a lot of time and useless questioning."

"I'll do my best, sir."

"Sure you will. All set, Joe?" Bradley glanced at the cop in the doorway.

"Come along, kid."

They went into the hall. In the wall outside the waiting room was one of those glass slits of the kind that used to decorate speakeasy doors. One-way vision. Bradley looked through into the room beyond.

"All right, young fellow. Just walk in and sit down. Stay as long as you want. Be absolutely sure that you do or don't recognize one or more of them before you come out."

"Yes, sir."

Bradley stationed himself by the peephole. He watched the boy go in and sit down, rolling his hat nervously in his fingers. Johnny and Pat sat in one corner of the room together. Linda Marsh, looking annoyed, was talking earnestly with George Pelham. Miss Devon apparently didn't believe in wasting time, even during a murder investigation. She had brought along the blue sock.

The rest of the room was peopled with stooges supplied by Joe.

"He's a conscientious guy," muttered Monahan at Bradley's elbow. "I'd either know or not know in about ten seconds."

"Better to have him sure," said Bradley.

At last the boy rose and walked out of the room. He joined Bradley and Monahan in the hall.

"Well, kid?"

The boy was sweating. "There's one of them there all right," he said. "I couldn't be wrong about her."

"Now we're getting places, Monahan said.

"Which one is it, son?"

"The old lady," said the boy. "I'd know her anywhere."

Bradley's eyes were bleak. "Let's be certain about this," he said. "Which one?"

"The one in the dark blue hat with the red berries on it."

Bradley's eyes shifted again to the peephole, and the sound he made under his breath was not happy.

"Take a look through here, son. Is it the one who's reading the newspaper now?"

"That's her," said the boy. "I'd know her anywhere."

"Okay, son, Run along back to your job."

"So it's Miss Devon!" Monahan said.

Bradley turned away from the peephole and started for his office. "Whenever I have nightmares," he said to Monahan, "the central figure is always an eyewitness. Our young friend has selected with great positiveness Mrs. Fogarty, best policewoman on the force, who wasn't within miles of Severied's apartment this morning."

14

I would like to say just this much, Inspector," said Linda Marsh. She stood facing Bradley across his desk. "I don't believe you have the right to drag people around the city against their will. Unless you had grounds on which to arrest me, which obviously you hadn't, you have exceeded your authority. I intend to see to it that you are disciplined."

"If you felt your rights were being violated," said Bradley, "you needn't have come."

"And have that fat-headed assistant of yours carry me bodily out of the office?"

Bradley chuckled.

"He's the kind who takes orders literally," Linda said. "You told him to bring me, and he'd have done it!"

"Well, now that you're here, Miss Marsh …"

"Now that I'm here, I'm not talking without the advice of my lawyer. If I'm to be treated like a suspect, I should have the privileges of a suspect."

"You sound as though you thought the idea was ridiculous," said Bradley.

"What idea?"

"Suspecting you of murder."

"Good heavens, man, didn't I make it quite clear to you last night that I was willing to co-operate? I don't think it was insane of me to expect a little consideration in return. I feel as George does. We've told you all we know. If you suspect us, place us under arrest. If you don't, stop pushing us around."

"I could arrest you, you know," said Bradley.

"What?" Linda's eyes widened.

"Sure I could. You were in all the places the murderer had to be. And certainly substituting the letter would have been duck soup for you, Miss Marsh. You would have been very smart, under those conditions, to have sent for me at once. That would have thrown suspicion entirely away from you."

"You're not being serious?" said Linda, who seemed to have forgotten about lawyers.

"Of course I'm serious. You had the opportunity. In one phase of the crime you had the best opportunity of all. You make a grade-A suspect, Miss Marsh."

"But, Mr. Bradley, I ..."

"What were you doing this morning, say from quarter of nine on?"

"Why ... I had breakfast about eight and got ready to go to the shop. Even though it's Sunday, I had arranged to see my foreign buyer there. I left my apartment about ... well, a few minutes before nine and walked down Fifth Avenue. I guess I did a little window-shopping, because it was going on quarter to ten when I let myself into the office. My appointment was for ten."

"Meet anybody on the avenue you knew?"

"No."

"See?" said Bradley, with a smile.

"See what?"

"No alibi," said Bradley. "How do I know you were window

shopping? How do I know you didn't take a taxi to Severied's apartment, knock off Douglas Prayne, and then get back to your store in time to keep your appointment?"

Linda's mouth opened in astonishment. "And how am I supposed to have gotten into Guy's apartment?" she said,

"Oh, that's simple. Gloria Prayne probably had a key. We didn't find it among her belongings. When you killed her you took the key, thinking you might want to use it later." Bradley regarded her stunned expression with pleasure. "Makes a nice little case, doesn't it?"

"But … but it's completely circumstantial!" Linda said. "Do people actually get railroaded on that kind of evidence?"

"Not often. I was just trying to show you how nice I've been not to arrest you."

"Inspector, I'm afraid I was a hit touchy when I first walked in here. I apologize."

"That's better," said Bradley. "Now sit down and tell me how long you've been in love with George Pelham."

"Mr. Bradley!" Color welled up from her throat and into her face.

"It's like pulling teeth," said Bradley, "to get you to give me credit for any intelligence."

Linda sat down. "I think," she said, "that I'm rattled."

"Best approved detective method," said Bradley. "Get 'em off balance and they tell all."

"What do you want to know?"

"What sort of a fellow is George Pelham?"

"I should have thought you'd know by now?"

"Perhaps I should," said Bradley. "I've seen him ride a horse. I've seen that he has patience and perseverance. Those are qualities our murderer had to have. But the captain wears a false face in public, Miss Marsh. The disappearance of his wife has changed him. The real man isn't quite as easy to get at as I could wish."

"George is one of the grandest guys in the world."

"Are you going to marry him?"

"Really!"

"Well, it's not such a foolish question. When I see an attractive young woman with decided maternal instincts for an interesting, tragic, and very eligible widower … two and two make four."

"I think," said Linda after a slight hesitation, "that if George asked me to marry him I would. But he never has, Inspector, and he never will. Dorothy was his one woman. The rest of us haven't much chance."

"You've been to Pelham's apartment often, I suppose."

"Of course. George and I are great friends. Why shouldn't I visit him?"

"No reason at all. I just wondered if you'd had the opportunity to find out if he owns a gun — an automatic, preferably."

"I … I think he does," Linda said. "Yes, I know he does. He had it in the war. He … he kept it along with his other trophies."

"That's all for now, Miss Marsh," said Bradley.

Linda didn't move. "Just a moment, Inspector. There is only one reason why George would ever kill a man or a woman. If he found out that someone was responsible for Dorothy's disappearance, he would take the law into his own hands."

"I can think of another reason," said Bradley.

Miss Devon settled herself in the chair by Bradley's desk. A ball of blue yarn rolled away across the floor, and the inspector retrieved it for her. Then the steel needles went to work.

"Most interesting Sunday morning I've spent in years," she observed, "Such unusual types in your waiting room."

"All cops," said Bradley. "I had a young man in there trying to pick out visitors to Severied's apartment."

"Success?" Miss Devon's tone was completely casual.

"He gave me a bad turn. I thought he'd picked on you. It turned out he had selected one of our people who, of course, was never there. Not helpful."

Miss Devon yanked a length of yarn loose from the ball. She spoke without looking up. "I think I can guess what you're going to ask me. What time I went shopping, why it took me nearly an hour, why I hadn't prepared for Sunday's housekeeping in advance, and if I know why Douglas went to Guy's apartment,"

"They'll do for starters," Bradley smiled.

"I went out about ten minutes after Douglas. It took me an hour because I went for a walk. I prefer thinking alone! The reason I had to shop was that we had meant to go on a bust today. Celebrate the Horse Show. The plan rather petered out, as you can imagine. I got what I could from the delicatessen, *after* I'd taken my walk!" She looked Bradley in the eye. "I could easily have gone to Guy's apartment, killed Douglas, and then done my shopping in the time I was out."

"I'll make a note of it," Bradley said.

"As to why Douglas went to Guy's apartment, I haven't the remotest idea. Or perhaps I'm not being truthful. Douglas didn't give any hint as to why he might want to see Guy, but perhaps I have had *notions* about it."

"Such as?"

"Damn!" said Miss Devon. "Did you ever turn a heel? If you don't count properly you're lost!" she began counting.

"Your notions," Bradley prompted.

"Oh, that!" Miss Devon let the sock drop to her lap. "Has the idea of blackmail ever entered your head in connection with this case, Mr. Bradley?"

"Lady, you're wasting your time keeping house," Bradley said. "There's a job open for you here any time you want it."

"I'll keep that in mind. The way things are going, I may not have any family to keep house for soon."

"There are only two people, so far involved in the case, who are well enough heeled to be worth blackmailing," Bradley said. "Severied and Miss Marsh."

"How right you are, Inspector."

"Following this blackmail theory," said Bradley, "and I have thought about it seriously for reasons that seem also to have occurred to you, Severied is our murderer."

"Why?"

"We assume Gloria was doing the blackmailing, don't we?"

"Of course!"

"Gloria got frightened into writing a letter incriminating her victim, and left it with Miss Marsh. Now, if Miss Marsh were the victim, she wouldn't have been given the letter to keep."

"Which narrows it down to Guy," said Miss Devon. "I'm quite certain, Mr. Bradley, that Guy was being blackmailed ... and the price was high! He had to marry the girl!"

"That's the way it looks."

"But you haven't sent out an alarm for Guy," said Miss Devon shrewdly. "And you're still questioning us. I should think any policeman in his right mind would concentrate on finding Guy."

"Maybe I'm not in my right mind," said Bradley.

"Oh, yes, you are! And I see it just as you do. Guy was being blackmailed, but not on his own account. He was paying out to protect someone else."

"That job is definitely yours," said Bradley.

"And who would Guy be likely to protect so earnestly in this setup?" Miss Devon went on relentlessly. "Why, George—his best friend!"

"And what has the captain got to hide in his life?" Bradley asked.

"Ah, there you have me! But" — and she paused for effect — "Guy was in no personal danger at Gloria's hands. The person he was protecting was the one who had something to fear."

"Quite," said Bradley.

Miss Devon's steady eyes met his. "It's been nice solving the case with you, Inspector," she said.

***

After Miss Devon had returned to the waiting room Bradley crossed to the windows and stood scowling down at the street, hands sunk deep in his pockets. After a time he came back to his desk and picked up the phone.

"Locate the telephone number of Captain George Pelham's apartment," he ordered, "and call it. Snyder is there. I want to talk to him."

He prowled up and down the room; but when the phone rang, it was still the headquarters operator.

"We've kept calling the number, Inspector, but there's no answer."

"Damn!" said Bradley. "Rube probably thinks it's someone for Pelham. See if the apartment house has a switchboard. Get hold of someone there to go upstairs and tell Rube to report in at once."

"Yes, sir."

This time the wait seemed endless. When the call came, Bradley spoke impatiently.

"Hello, Rube?"

"Yeah, this is Rube." The sergeant's voice sounded queer. "Thanks for phonin' the super, Red."

"What the hell's wrong with you?"

"Listen, Red, Pelham's still at headquarters, ain't he?"

"Of course he is."

"Well, get a load of this," said Rube bitterly. "I get the key for this dump from the super, and I come upstairs. I walk into the apartment and ... wham! Someone clouts me over the back of the head!"

"Who, Rube?"

"How should I know? I never get a look at him. Fireworks go off in front of my eyes, and the next thing I know the super is bendin' over me and I'm lyin' on the floor with my head on a pillow."

"With *what?"*

"That's right. After he knocks me cold this guy puts a pillow under my head, the polite — "

Bradley was choking with laughter.

"Okay, giggle your fool head off!" Rube said heatedly. "But it's ten to one there ain't any gun here now."

"I'm afraid you're right, Rube. Take a quick look and then come on downtown. I'm about to have a talk with the captain. Maybe he'll be a nice boy and tell me the truth about his toys."

***

Pelham stood in front of the desk looking at Bradley.

"Sorry, but I'll have to keep you waiting a moment, Captain. Sit down." Bradley was thumbing through a sheaf of papers.

Pelham sat down. The nerve at the corner of his mouth would not stay still. He would have been astonished if he could have seen the paper which Bradley was studying with such evident concentration. It was a notice of the annual precinct Christmas party for the benefit of the families of sick policemen.

The captain was getting the "silent treatment." As the minutes passed, he kept crossing and uncrossing his legs and tugging at the end of his mustache. Finally Bradley folded his papers neatly and put them to one side. He gave Pelham a level look.

"All right, Captain, let's get down to brass tacks. Why did you murder your wife?"

Before Bradley could lift a hand, Pelham had lunged across the intervening space and was at his throat.

15

BRADLEY's swivel chair crashed against the wall. For a second he was in a decidedly tough spot, as Pelham's fingers dug into his windpipe. Then he managed to get one leg raised and to plant his foot squarely in the middle of Pelham's stomach. He shoved off, and Pelham went spinning across the room.

"Cut it!" Bradley said. The forward impetus of the shove had brought him to his feet.

The captain rushed him, and the result was short but sweet. Bradley side-stepped and his right fist came up under Pelham's chin, snapping his head back and ending the rush. Pelham's knees wobbled, and he went down and lay still.

Bradley, feeling gingerly of his throat, walked to the office door.

"Joe!" he called.

The uniformed cop bustled in. He gaped when he caught sight of Pelham, "Holy Mother, Red, what happened?"

"I guess I didn't smile when I said it, Joe."

"He jumped you?"

"And not just for the records," said Bradley. "He really did. Take his feet. We'll sit him over there on that chair."

Bradley loosened Pelham's collar and got water from the cooler. Pelham was stirring as Bradley held the cup to his lips. Then Pelham opened his eyes, and Bradley saw the dark rage burning in them.

"I'll stick around, Red," said Joe.

Pelham gripped the arms of the chair and tried to pull himself erect. Bradley rested his fingers against Pelham's chest. Pelham sat down.

"You're outnumbered Pelham," Bradley said. "Take it easy."

Pelham wet his lips. His voice was cracked and hoarse. "So help me God, Bradley, if it's the last thing I ever do I'll make you pay for that crack, you dirty ward-heeler."

Bradley looked pained. "Whenever anyone has it in for a cop, they accuse him of being a politician," he said to Joe.

Pelham stood up. Bradley had dropped back into his own chair and he made no effort to stop him, but Joe closed in.

"You better not start anything, Mister," Joe said.

"You accused me of murder," Pelham said.

"If you'd let me finish," said Bradley, "I might have accused you of several."

"In view of that charge," Pelham said, "I'm not talking. I'm going to …"

"Don't tell me," said Bradley, "let me guess. You're going to send for your lawyer. Prayne had that idea. Miss Marsh had that idea. I'm getting tired of it, Captain. It's like a factory owner getting a night watchman to watch his night watchman! I'm a public servant, Pelham, paid by you and a few million other taxpayers. I'm supposed to be on your side. If you're guilty, by all means send for your lawyer. I wouldn't want to talk to you under any other conditions. But if you're not guilty—"

"You seem to have made up your mind on that point," said Pelham.

"If your wife wasn't murdered, what did happen to her?"

"Why, damn you, Bradley, I'm not here to answer questions about Dorothy! I went to the police when I was in trouble, and a hell of a lot of good it did me. They stalled and fooled around and finally gave up the case. Why should I help you disguise the fact that you're not competent to handle the present situation?"

"Where is your old army automatic?" Bradley asked.

"If you're so damned anxious to know, get a search warrant and go over my apartment."

"I have. It isn't there!"

Pelham's eyes flickered, and then his lips clamped together.

"Prayne was murdered with the same type of gun as yours."

"How do you know that?"

"A Colt automatic."

"Then, for cripe's sake, arrest me!"

"What time did you leave your apartment this morning?"

"After breakfast."

"Did you go directly from your apartment to the Crop and Spur?"

"What good will it do me to say yes or no? I can't prove it."

Bradley sighed and leaned back in his chair, breaking the tempo of the inquisition.

"I've got a lot of time, Pelham," he said. "I can wait indefinitely for you to cool off. I'm convinced your wife's disappearance and these two murders are connected. I repeat, if your wife wasn't murdered what did happen to her?"

"Ask the brilliant officer who was in charge of the case for the police! He put mc on that rack at the time. Perhaps you can drag some facts out of thin air that he couldn't."

"Was your wife in love with somebody else, Pelham?"

"I ought to kill you for that," said Pelham in a low voice.

"Maybe you killed *her* for it!"

Pelham started forward, fists clenched but Joe pushed him

back into the chair. "And what about her body?" Pelham raged, "I suppose I flushed it down the drains!"

"It's been done," said Bradley coolly.

"You —"

The swivel chair hinge creaked as Bradley continued rocking gently. "How was it? Did Gloria and her father have some inkling of the truth? Is that why you had to get rid of them?"

Pelham laughed, a mirthless rasping sound. "I'm a mass killer, Inspector! I'm out to get the whole family! They know where the … the skeleton is in my closet. They …" His voice rose hysterically.

"Get him some more water, Joe," said Bradley. He fished his pipe from his pocket and filled it from the crock on the desk. He kept his eyes on Pelham, who drank the water Joe brought him and then crumpled the paper cup.

"Has Guy Severied got a key to your apartment?" Bradley asked.

"What of it?"

"Nothing … except that he's just been there and slugged one of my men over the head."

"Seriously, I hope!"

"Now, now, Captain, that's not up to snuff. Definitely not funny."

"Am I supposed to be overwhelmed with sympathy for you bunglers?"

"How are you on sympathy for Gloria and Douglas Prayne?"

"That's a trick question of the kindergarten variety," Pelham said. "Why don't you warn me that anything I say will be used against me?"

"I'm not the only one who suspects you of murder, Pelham. Your best friend was so worried he hotfooted it to your apartment just in order to see if your gun was there."

"Why should Guy do that?"

"To protect you."

"From what, for God's sake!"

"Apparently he doesn't want to see you burn for what he considers justifiable homicide. Protecting you is his best trick. He's been paying blackmail for a long time to guard your secret."

"The man's insane!" Pelham cried. "What secret?"

"The secret of your wife's disappearance. It got a little too hot when Gloria actually put it down on paper and gave it to Linda Marsh to keep. You couldn't risk that, could you, Captain?"

In spite of Joe, Pelham struggled to his feet. "Bradley, if you know what happened to my wife, out with it! All the rest of this gibberish of yours … it's bluff, and you know it. But if you've facts about Dorothy, tell me what they are. I've a right to the truth!"

"That's what I'm supposed to be getting out of you, Pelham."

"All you want is an arrest," Pelham charged. "Why don't you investigate the facts? If you checked on my movements last night, you'd know I never left the Garden … that I couldn't have because of the horses. Shea will back that up. Outside of half an hour at suppertime I was never away from the Garden basement."

"That would have been time enough."

"Am I the best fall guy you can find to satisfy the commissioner?"

"You're an awful good one," said Bradley. He looked at Joe. "Take him away," he said.

"Arrest me!" Pelham shouted. "Lock me up! Turn loose your thugs on me! Maybe you could beat a confession out of me! Maybe …"

"Take him away," Bradley repeated sharply.

Joe took Pelham's arm and led him, still raging, to the door.

"And, Joe" — Bradley was scowling at the lamp shade; reached out to straighten it—"turn the lot of 'em free. Tell 'em I don't want them anymore."

"What's wrong, Inspector?" Pelham sneered. "Didn't the blitzkrieg work?"

"I oughta bat your teeth in," Joe growled,

Bradley seemed to have forgotten them. He had swung his chair around and was staring out the window.

***

Inspector Flynn of the Missing Persons Bureau greeted Bradley with enthusiasm. Flynn had once been an active member of the Homicide Division, but a knee shattered in a gun fight in the prohibition era had relegated him to desk work.

"You're the last guy in the world I expected to see this day, Luke," he said.

"Not snow, nor rain, nor heat, nor gloom of night," murmured Bradley.

"I've just heard of the lollapalooza you're mixed up in," Flynn said.

"And that's what brings me here, Mickey. I want help."

"Name your poison."

"I want the records on the case of one Dorothy Pelham, who disappeared about five years ago."

"Did we find her?"

"No. But I understand the case was officially dropped."

"Sit down and take a load off your feet," Flynn invited. "I'll dig up the files for you."

It took about fifteen minutes, and then Flynn limped back into his office with a brown cardboard folder. Bradley opened it. On top of the pile of reports was a studio photograph of Dorothy Pelham.

“Nifty-lookin’ dish,” said Flynn.

“I’d heard she was beautiful,” Bradley said. “She really was, and no kidding.”

The record was complete if concise. The case had been reported in June of 1935 by Captain George Pelham, the missing woman’s husband. He had just returned from a motor trip through the New England States where he had been on business.

Inspector Earl Williams was assigned to the case on the seventeenth.

Inspector Williams’ first report was brief:

> Dorothy Pelham, the missing woman, has been married lo George Pelham, ex-Captain of engineers in the A.E.F. for about four years. Pelham is connected with the Thoroughbred Race Horse Breeding Association of America as a sort of traveling secretary. He went out of town on the 11th, covering race tracks and farms in Massachusetts and Rhode Island. Purpose, to make some sort of report to the association.
>
> He returned on the 15th, evening. Dorothy Pelham was not at home. No evidence of an intended absence. Clothes, jewels, etc., intact. Only possible evidence she might have intended staying away was absence of toothbrush. Too slender. Might have thrown it away with intention of buying another while she was out.
>
> Employees in apartment building saw her go out afternoon of 12th. Said nothing about going away. Cheerful and pleasant as usual. These are the last-known persons to have seen Mrs. Pelham. Pelham reports phoning all friends, acquaintances of his wife. Blank.

Then the second report, much briefer:

> Hospitals, public and private, morgues covered. Blank. Followed up all reported accidents to females since 11th. Blank. No reports of suicides at water front or on ferry runs.

The third report:

> Talked with nearly fifty friends of Dorothy Pelham. Every one of them scoffs at notion of suicide or willful disappearance. Subject was gay, full of life, no evidence of family trouble. She and husband out in society a lot, but evidently very happy.

The fourth report:

> Investigated possibility of homicide. No known motive for anyone. Checked husband's alibi.

Here Bradley's eyes narrowed and he read closely.

> George Pelham at Boston, Greenfield, Narragansett, Providence, registered at hotels in each city. Impossible to get complete detailed alibi, but seems unlikely he is involved, He could have flown to New York and back again to any one of these points in the course of an evening, but no record of such a trip. Checked with regular commercial air lines. Blank. There are hundreds of private planes he could have chartered. Take months to check them all. Advise against expenses, since there is no real reason to suspect him.

The fifth report.

> Gave Pelham the works. Thoroughly convinced he is innocent of any crime. Close to mental collapse, or I'm nuts.

The rest was completely negative. Nothing turned up to give Inspector Williams the slightest lead. The case was dropped in December. The only other piece of information was a note to the effect that the Bonesteel Detective Agency, private, had been engaged by Pelham to carry on the search.

"What are you looking for?" Flynn asked.

"Evidence of murder," said Bradley mournfully. "Nothing very hopeful here."

"Don't look like it."

"Mickey, I'd like to talk to Inspector Williams. Can you get him down here today to see me?"

Flynn shook his head. "That I can't," he said. "Williams is retired. Got a farm somewhere up in Westchester County, I hear."

"Can you get his address?"

"Sure. Some of the boys will have it."

"The pension clerk will know," Bradley suggested.

***

The commissioner drew circles and curlicues on the yellow scratch-pad at his elbow.

He looked worried.

"I don't like it, Bradley," he said, "I don't like it one damn bit!"

Bradley was slumped in a red leather armchair by the commissioner's desk. He had just struck a match, and he let the flame burn halfway down the stick before he applied it to his pipe.

"Not a nice case," he conceded.

"It'll be plastered all over the front pages tomorrow You were lucky to miss the bulk of the Sunday papers."

"We've been in the papers before, Commissioner," Bradley shrugged.

The commissioner's expression was pensive. "You know I've always been an admirer of yours, Bradley. Your record speaks for itself. I'd let you go farther with your own methods than any other man on the force."

"Thank you, Mr. Commissioner,"

"But, damn it" — and the point of the commissioner's pencil snapped — "the way you're going about this seems goofy to me. You keep stressing the connection between these murders and the disappearance of Dorothy Pelham. But where's the evidence to point to it, man?"

"I don't believe in coincidence," said Bradley.

"My dear Inspector ..."

"Look here, sir. There are two kinds of coincidence, the kind you can explain and the kind you can't. If I'm walking along Fifth Avenue at nine in the morning and I meet you on the corner of Forty-Third Street, and then the next morning the same thing happens, we call it coincidence. But we can explain it. You get into the Grand Central each morning at eight-fifty and you walk across town. So it isn't strange, really, my bumping into you. That's the garden variety of coincidence. But there's another kind."

"Well?"

"Suppose a young fellow takes a girl out driving in his car. They go up a steep, mountain road. The young fellow stops his car because he thinks he has a flat. He gets out to look. While he's out of the car, the brake gives way, the car goes over an embankment, and the girl is killed."

"What's this got to do with ... "

"Wait a minute, sir. Now suppose that same young fellow, four or five years later, takes another girl driving over a mountain road and stops because he thinks he has a flat. And suppose again, while he's out of the car, the brake gives way, the car goes over an embankment, and the girl is killed."

"Well?"

"Would you accept that as a tragic coincidence, Mr. Commissioner, or would you, like me, say 'that's too damned fishy to swallow?"

"Well, that would be a bit thick, Bradley. But ..."

"I think it's a bit thick, sir, that in this same group the same thing has happened twice, with only the variation of discovering the body the second time. If nothing else, the first crime — and I believe it was a crime — gave the murderer a pattern for the second. The shooting of Douglas Prayne was apparently an emergency measure. Until I've run it to earth and proved, I'm wrong, I'll still be convinced that Dorothy Pelham's disappearance is tied into this affair tight as a drum!"

"Then why not make an arrest?" the commissioner demanded.

"Who shall I arrest, sir?"

"Pelham or Severied or both."

"On what evidence?"

"It's a moral certainty that Prayne was shot with Pelham's gun."

Bradley smiled faintly. "Juries have a way of rejecting moral certainties, sir."

"But Pelham's got no alibi!"

"Neither has anyone else on my list. There's just one person I'll put in the clear beyond a shadow of doubt, Patricia Prayne."

"Not the Curtin boy?"

"I'm pretty sure about him, Commissioner. But from the standpoint of alibis he's in bad. He discovered both bodies, and we only have his word for it that he was just unlucky. As for the rest, if I could hook a motive onto any one of them, I could make a pinch."

The commissioner didn't seem any happier. "Well, that brings me to the last point. Why in the name of God haven't you sent out an alarm for Severied? He deliberately gave your man the slip last night. He's obviously in hiding or he would have come forward. It's practically certain he's the one who slugged Sergeant Snyder. Why haven't you got every cop on the force looking for him?"

Bradley was silent, puffing methodically on his pipe. At last he said, "What will happen if I arrest him? I might charge him with assault. There was no crime in giving Monahan the slip. He wasn't under arrest or orders to stay in his apartment. It's suspicious, sure. But a half-hour alter I lock him up, his lawyer will have him out. I wouldn't like that."

"Bradley, what in tarnation … "

"Mr. Commissioner, I've a number of hunches. One of them has to do with Severied. I don't know where he is … true. But neither does the murderer."

"But it's damn likely that Severied *is* the murderer!"

"I don't think so, sir. And as long as he chooses to stay hidden it suits me. Because" — and Bradley heaved a deep sigh — "I believe if the murderer gets the opportunity, *Guy Severied will be his next victim!*"

16

THE commissioner stared at Bradley. Then he spoke in a soothing voice.

"That sounds like the end of a chapter in a detective story!" he said. "You don't have to keep me in suspense, you know."

"I don't want to, Commissioner. The case has taken on a kind of shape, sir, and I'll give it to you as far as it goes. I think Gloria Prayne was indulging in blackmail. If you consider the letter, and the implications of her visit to Linda Marsh, you'll see why. In the group are only two who have anything to be blackmailed out of … Severied and Miss Marsh. Since the letter was left with Miss Marsh to turn over to the police in case something went wrong, that makes it Severied."

"But that's all the more reason why you should … "

"Let me finish, sir. Severied knew that letter was in Miss Marsh's keeping. Drunk as he was, the moment he heard of the murder he made straight for Miss Marsh. He did his best to dissuade us from opening it."

"But …"

"When you're blackmailing, Commissioner, you have to make it evident to the victim that he can't slide off the hook by silencing you. Therefore Gloria told Severied what she'd done. But … and here's the big but, sir. When we refused to burn the letter, Severied gave up … resigned himself to our discovery of something unpleasant and damaging. See what that brings us to?"

"No, I don't."

"If the secret bad been anything ruinous to him, personally, he would have gone a lot further in his efforts to stop us. If he were the murderer, he would have known there was nothing in the letter and he wouldn't have made any fuss at all. So I conclude: (a) that he is not the murderer; (b) that he was paying blackmail not to protect himself, but someone else!"

"I see. It's smart reasoning, Bradley. No doubt of it."

Bradley continued, "There is one person whom Severied has been in the habit of helping and protecting for a long time. Pelham! I think — and now it's guesswork, sir — that when he heard about Gloria he jumped to the instant conclusion that it was Pelham who'd killed her. And I think this morning, when he heard about Prayne, he was still playing with that notion. That's why he, too, went to Pelham's apartment to see if the gun was there."

"But you think he took the gun, don't you?"

"No, I don't. I think he found it missing … just as we should have if we'd beaten him to the search."

"And you think he's prepared to protect Pelham, even against a murder charge?"

"I'm still guessing, Commissioner, but I don't think he's sure yet. I think the reason he's hiding is that he doesn't want to be forced to talk until he is sure. He's been willing to pay blackmail for a long time."

"But what secret is he keeping, Bradley? If he knows that Pelham murdered his wife, and he's covering for him, then he's an accessory."

"Perhaps murder isn't his secret. If I knew, this case would be on ice. But I feel this, sir. Severied has facts that we haven't. He's doing a bit of detective work of his own. I think if he finds that Pelham is guilty of murder he'll turn him in. I think if he finds Pelham is innocent he'll keep dodging until we hit on the truth and he can come into the clear without having to divulge his secret."

"You think then, that … "

"I think the story behind the blackmailing is the crux of the whole case, Commissioner. Severied knows it, and the murderer knows it. Right now Severied, in possession of that information, is much more dangerous to the murderer than we are. That's why I say he is logically the next victim. If we arrest him, bring him back into focus so that the murderer can get on his trail, we may have a third crime on our hands. As I see it, my job is to get hold of that secret if I can. Once I have it too, Severied's danger becomes instantly minimized. The murderer will have to worry about me then. And if he makes a move against me ... " Bradley's smile was grim. "I would like that, Commissioner, very much."

The commissioner nodded. "But this secret. It's so intangible! Where do you begin?"

Bradley knocked out his pipe. He sounded tired. "I've got a one-track mind, Commissioner. When I know more about Dorothy Pelham, I think I'll be on the way."

The commissioner drummed on the edge of his desk with his fingers. Then he made a decision. "Okay, you stubborn red-headed cluck! Handle it your own way. And good luck."

"Thank you, sir, I'm going to need it."

***

Mr. Jerry Bonesteel, private investigator, sat on a high stool in Al Muller's Restaurant and Bar adjoining Madison Square

Garden. Muller's is a hangout for everyone who has business at the Garden — fight managers and their charges, hockey players, rodeo performers, circus people; and during Horse Show week you'll see a good many dinner coats and top hats. Al Muller himself, short, stocky, shirt-sleeved host, who looks as if in his youth he might have been a wrestler or a gymnast, knows everyone, remembers everyone. In the late afternoon Muller's bar magically becomes decorated with slabs of rye bread and platters of cold meat. It is the nearest thing to the old-fashioned free lunch you can find in New York.

Mr. Jerry Bonesteel, nattily dressed in a double-breasted serge, a stiff-bosomed shirt with a large diamond stud, a crisp bow tie, and a carefully brushed derby hat, was availing himself of Herr Muller's largesse when Bradley's hand dropped on his shoulder. He turned on his stool.

"Why, you old son of a bitch!" he cried. "Where you been keeping yourself?"

"Around," said Bradley, occupying the next stool.

"Say, it's great to see you. It's great to see a guy in a nice clean business who doesn't have to chisel expense accounts to make a living."

"Business tough?"

"Terrible. About the only way you can get by is hiding under beds for evidence in divorce cases. It stinks. What are you doing here?"

"Looking for you."

"No kidding!"

"No kidding. I finally located one of your operatives who said you were apt to be here between five and six almost any day."

"Know why? They have the best damn salami in New York."

"I could bear to find out for myself," said Bradley. "And a

bottle of ale," he added to the bartender.

"What's on your mind, Red? Got a case?"

"Don't you read the papers?"

"Not if I can help it!" Then Bonesteel's eyebrows went up. "Not the Prayne case?"

"The Prayne case in person, Jerry."

"Oh, boy!"

"That's why I've been hunting for you."

"I don't get it"

"You know the Praynes, don't you?" Bradley was loading a piece of rye bread with salami. "In connection with the disappearance of Dorothy Pelham back in '35."

"So that's the way it is," said Bonesteel. He tapped his highball glass on the bar and slid it across to the bartender with a nod. "Double," he said.

Bradley munched his sandwich, indicated approval, and reached for his glass of ale.

"I'm a smart guy," said Bonesteel. "Mind like a steel trap. You're interested in Dorothy Pelham. You're homicide with a capital Hom. You think maybe little Dorothy might not have shuffled off to Buffalo of her own free will."

"I'd like to know what you think," Jerry." Bradley was watching the private detective in the mirror behind the bar. Bonesteel was looking thoughtfully into his drink.

"Nothing to it, Red," he said after a pause. "Mind you, I wasn't hired to investigate a crime. Just to find the gal."

"Uh-huh," said Bradley.

"But the department went into that," Bonesteel said quickly. "Bird named Williams was in charge. He dug around quite a lot and then washed it up. Nothing against anyone."

Bradley arranged two fresh pieces of salami on a slice of bread, making certain that the entire surface was covered. "Retired now."

"That's right. He's got a farm in Peekskill. I stopped off there last summer to see him. He'd asked me to a long time ago."

"Nice place?"

"A top-notch dairy farm," said Bonesteel, looking away. "Must have cost him a lot of dough."

"Thanks," said Bradley quietly. "About Dorothy Pelham?"

"Red, I'm not really a chiseler at heart. I shagged around for nearly three months trying to find some kind of a lead, and then I went to Severied and told him, frankly, he was wasting his dough."

"Severied?"

"Sure, Guy Severied, the society sportsman. He's the one who hired me and paid my fee. He was a buddy of the gal's husband."

"You must have found out something of interest in three months," said Bradley.

"I did. I found out I'd like to work for Severied for life. That bird never once checked an expense account, Red."

"Nice kind of a fellow, huh?"

"A prince."

Bradley sighed. "About Dorothy?"

"Red, that gal just went up in smoke. That's on the level. If you think there was dirty work, I'm sorry, but I can't tell you a thing to back it up."

Bradley drained his glass. "Well, there was no harm in asking you." He slid off the stool and handed the bartender a five-dollar bill. "It's all on me," he said.

"Gee, Red, thanks. Wish I could have helped you," Bonesteel said. He was frowning.

"I wish you could. Well, so long, Jerry."

"So long."

Bradley started for the door.

"Red!" Bonesteel called after him.

Bradley turned.

The private detective avoided the stare of his level gray eyes. “There’s one thing you might not know about Dotty Pelham.”

“Yes?”

Bonesteel gave his bow tie a straightening tug. “She was crazy about the boys, Red.”

Bradley waited for more, but Bonesteel had turned back to his bread and salami.

17

"WELL, Julius, doesn't that prove that your friend is wrong?" Pelham demanded. "Doesn't that clear the lot of us?"

They had all come back from headquarters together to find Mr. Julius waiting for them at the Prayne apartment. The old man had told them what he wanted — a set of alibis which could either take them all off Bradley's list of suspects or point a finger at one of them specifically.

"An alibi must be checked and tested before it stands up," said the old man, thumbing through a stack of notes written in his spidery hand.

"But on the face of it …" Pelham began.

"On the face of it," said the old man sourly, "you are all pure as the driven snow. But anyone can invent a plausible story. After I've checked …" He shrugged.

"How long will it take?"

"Few days … a week … two weeks. Depends on how much you've lied."

"Good God!" Pelham groaned. "By that time Bradley will have dragged us all to hell and gone!" He crossed over to the sideboard and poured himself a drink. The neck of the decanter clicked against the rim of his glass.

"George … please, sweet. You musn't let this get you," Linda said.

"For God's sake, what do you expect? Bradley's sunk … hasn't got a real lead in the case. So what does he do? Starts prying into the past … into Dorothy's disappearance. It'll make a field day for the press, and take the heat off him a little while he stumbles around looking for a trustworthy clue."

"Bradley's no superman," said Mr. Julius. "He can't get anywhere without help. You're not helping. No one is."

"How can we help?" Pelham asked. "The man's up in the clouds like a balloon. He's developed a romantic theory and doesn't bother with facts."

"What facts?"

Pelham banged his glass down on the table, "There must be facts … clues! Why dig up old scandals … open old wounds? I tell you it's a smoke screen to hide his helplessness."

"It's so cruel, so useless," Linda said. "To accuse George deliberately of murdering Dorothy, when everyone knows …"

"Knows what?" said Mr. Julius.

"Why, how much George loved her!"

"It's going back pretty far," Johnny said. He was sitting beside Pat on the couch. "Personally, I think …"

"No one cares a hoot what you think," said Mr. Julius. He was peering at Pelham from beneath shaggy eyebrows. "You mentioned facts, George. I still say, what facts?"

"Well, what do detectives usually find? Fingerprints clues … evidence."

"Oh, that!" said Mr. Julius.

"What else do you have on which to base an investigation?"

"People," said Mr. Julius promptly.

"But, Uncle Julius, if these alibis you've collected …" Pat said.

"Don't count on 'em. Even if they check. Until Bradley finds out where Gloria was killed, alibis won't amount to a hill of beans."

"He'll never find that out," said Pelham.

"You know that?" Mr. Julius' eyebrows rose.

"Of course I don't *know* it. But from the way he goes about things, I'd say it was unlikely."

"Would you, indeed," said the old man.

"But there *are* facts, George," said Celia Devon, looking up from her knitting. "Guy, for instance, is a fact. He's missing. He seems concerned about you. He was at your apartment and had to knock out Sergeant Snyder to get away."

"That's only guesswork," Pelham said, "Guy is missing, so Guy is blamed for slugging Snyder. Who saw him? How do they know it wasn't a burglar?"

"Or Santa Claus," said Mr. Julius.

Miss Devon continued, undisturbed, "I don't think it's a state secret that Gloria was blackmailing Guy. That explains why he was so unhappy about marrying her. Gloria wrote a letter containing incriminating information and left it with Linda. That's why she was killed, it is probably why Douglas also was killed. Those are facts, George."

"And where do they get you?"

"Not far. But they explain Mr. Bradley's interest in your past, in all our pasts. He's trying to put his finger on a fact so important two people have been murdered to keep it."

"Celia, for God's sake! That's nonsense!"

"Is it, George?"

"If that's so, Miss Devon," Johnny said, "Guy is guilty. He was being blackmailed; he's taken it on the lam. And yet Bradley seems to make no effort to find him."

"Hasn't it occurred to you why?"

"No, it hasn't."

"Guy isn't hiding because he's guilty. He's hiding because he doesn't want to tell the facts he knows. I'd do the same thing. I'd stay somewhere I was quite certain this murderer couldn't find me."

"Aunt Celia!"

"It's not a pleasant notion," said Miss Devon, "but I have no doubt that one of us in this room is a murderer. I don't mind saying I wish I were with Guy."

There was a silence, broken at last by Mr. Julius' chuckle. "Nice running with the ball, Celia!" he said.

Miss Devon ignored him. "We might just as well face it. Pat, you're trying to find a weakness in Bradley's case. But suppose, while you search for it, you come on a truth … a dangerous truth. This person, whom you love, whom you can't believe guilty of evil, will turn on you. It's not safe for us to pry and search. Leave it to Bradley. I have confidence in him. He doesn't jump at the obvious."

"Celia, I'm with Pat," Linda Marsh said. "I simply can't believe that one of us … "

Pat was silent, staring at her hands.

"Heaven knows I'm sorry for the murderer," said Miss Devon, in a calm, matter-of-fact tone. "Fear has driven him to it, he must be going through a hell of his own. But he is dangerous. When a dog you've loved goes mad, it may break your heart; but you shoot him. That is what we face. A mad dog … a sick mind. We can't expect him to act toward tm or feel about us as he did before this blight descended on him."

"But Aunt Celia … "

"Since this madness doesn't show on the surface, Bradley must look for the causes of it. That, George, is why he is interested in Dorothy's disappearance. In a set of otherwise normal lives it is a high-pressure incident, a time of stress which may have started the warping of a mind."

She looked searchingly around at them. No one moved or spoke except Julius, who was nodding his head sagely.

"One of us knows that secret," Miss Devon said, "and the keeping of it has become an obsession … so great an obsession that he is willing to kill and keep on killing to protect it. The rest of us … we can't keep our minds still if we wish. The seed is planted. We are remembering Dorothy, wondering what there was about it that seemed unimportant at the time which might now have some significance."

"Celia, why should any facts have been withheld?" Pelham protested. "And if there were, why didn't the police or the private detectives ever come across a single clue to them?"

"I don't know, George. But there is a secret, Guy knows it. One of you knows it. Guy's been willing to pay to guard it, and I think he's praying Bradley will catch the murderer without his having to tell."

The color slowly faded from Pelham's face. "You keep saying 'he,' Celia? Are you, too, accusing me of murder?"

"I am not accusing anyone," said Miss Devon. "You spoke about facts. I was trying to show you that there are some, and that Mr. Bradley has them well in hand."

"But if you're right, Aunt Celia," said Pat, "then Guy must be in danger … very real danger."

"He's not playing hide and seek to win his letter," snapped Mr. Julius.

George Pelham drew a deep breath. "I'm going to find him," he said. "Guy and I have stood together through everything. If it's something about Dorothy, he'll tell me. He's never kept anything from me."

"George, wait!" Linda called after him, as he started for the door.

"If I were you, Linda," said Miss Devon, "I wouldn't go after him. I'd go home to my apartment, lock my door, and stay there till I heard Mr. Bradley had made an arrest."

Linda stood uncertainly in the middle of the room. They all heard the door close behind Pelham.

"There's only one person Guy would go to these lengths to protect," Miss Devon said.

"Not George!" Linda cried, "Celia, you mustn't say that! Mustn't think it!"

Pat was clinging tightly to Johnny's hand. She wasn't looking at Linda's white face.

Miss Devon smoothed out the wrinkles in her skirt. "Is anyone interested in supper?" she asked quietly.

18

AFTER dinner that night Bradley got his own car out of the garage and drove to Peekskill alone. A steady rain in the city turned to snow when he'd gotten as far as Ossining, and the going was slow. It was nearly eleven o'clock when, after getting directions at the Eagle Hotel, he turned off a back road into the driveway of Earl Williams' farm.

He caught a glimpse of the rambling stone farmhouse, and of lights still burning in a wing at the rear. He parked his car and walked around toward the back door. As he approached, a dog, on the inside, set up a terrific clamor. Bradley saw the shadow of someone moving quickly against the drawn window shade. Then he mounted the back steps and knocked.

The dog continued its barking, but for a long time no one came. It was not until after Bradley had knocked a second time that he heard a bolt shot back and the door was opened just enough for the man inside to peer out.

"Well?"

"Earl Williams?"

"Yes."

"I know it's late, but I'd like to talk with you for a few minutes,

I'm Luke Bradley, Homicide Division, New York City."

"Bradley!" No mistaking the startled note in the man's voice. Then the door opened wide. "Down Squire! Shut up!" The collie subsided, but kept a suspicious eye on Bradley. "Come in."

The kitchen was low-ceilinged, with heavy hand-hewn beams. The once-white woodwork had yellowed with smoke and steam from the coal range. There was a fire in the stove and the room was warm, the air thick with tobacco smoke. Bradley saw a calabash pipe lying on the scrubbed tabletop, a book turned face down, a cigarette stub burning in a saucer.

Williams was a tall, stoop-shouldered man with white hair, a leathery face, and deep-set black eyes.

"Mickey Flynn told me I'd find you up here," Bradley said. "Mind if I take off my coat and sit down?"

"Of course not. Let me help you." Williams acted like a man who was recovering from a blow between the eyes. He took Bradley's coat and hat and placed them on a chair. The collie sniffed at them and then came over and slipped a wet, cold nose into Bradley's open palm.

"Friends?" said Bradley.

Williams laughed uneasily. "He makes a great to-do when anyone comes around at night. But he's really very gentle."

"Great country dogs," said Bradley. He looked across the room at a door which opened into a dark corridor.

"Draft?" Williams started for the door.

"Oh, no. I'm quite comfortable, thanks."

Williams turned a straight-backed kitchen chair around and straddled it. He picked up his calabash, struck a match on the underside of the table. "How's Flynn, anyway?" he asked.

Bradley was looking at the cigarette in the saucer. It had almost burned itself away. "Oh, he's fine."

Williams fidgeted with the burnt match, waiting for Bradley to open the conversation. Bradley had begun loading his own pipe. He was in no hurry.

"Just driving through?" Williams asked finally.

"No. No, I came especially to see you, Earl." The inspector's tone was friendly.

"Oh, drive up from the city?"

"Yeah. Slow going. Headlights don't do so well when it's snowing." Bradley puffed contentedly at his pipe, his eyes roving around the room. "I suppose the old Dutch farmers used to live in their kitchens. Made 'em big enough."

"Yes … yes, I suppose they did. You said you came specially."

"Need help on a case," said Bradley. He rubbed the collie's head, and smoked.

"I've been reading the papers," Williams said. "You … you're handling the Prayne case, aren't you?"

"Yes."

"I knew them at one time," Williams said. He took a bandanna handkerchief from his hip pocket and ran it over his face. "Connection with a case of my own. Naturally I was interested in reading about what's happened. Is it … is it something about the Praynes you wanted to ask me?"

"No." Bradley said. "I wanted to ask you what really happened to Dorothy Pelham."

"Pelham? Why, that's the case I was talking about."

"Yes," said Bradley. The cigarette in the saucer had burned itself out completely, heaving the tapering gray ash.

"That case was never solved, Bradley. One of those things. I couldn't break it … no leads, no nothing."

"Bunk," said Bradley, and stroked the dog.

"I beg your pardon?"

"I said 'bunk,' " said Bradley, with a pleasant smile.

Williams sat perfectly still and silent for a moment, gripping the knobs on the back of the chair with both hands. "I think," he said, "if you were to read the records at headquarters …"

"I have read the records … word for word, and several times."

"Then …"

"The records don't tell me what I want to know."

"For example?" There was panic in Williams' dark eyes, but Bradley wasn't looking at him.

"For example," Bradley said, "the records don't show how you happened to buy this farm."

"Oh!"

"How did you?"

"Squire, come away. Stop being a nuisance," Williams said sharply to the dog.

"I like him," Bradley said. His fingers scratched behind the dog's ear, and Squire seemed about to swoon with delight. "About this place … "

"Why, that's simple. I had a chance to buy it at a very reasonable figure. I'd always wanted a farm. I decided—"

"Where did you get the money?"

"Now look, Bradley … "

"You didn't save it out of your pay as a detective. You were born in Brooklyn. You were on the force when you were twenty-two. You've never had any money. Yet you were able to buy this farm. Nine thousand, cash on the line, according to the local real-estate man.

Williams moistened his lips. "My wife … " he began.

"Your wife was Mary McInnes of Rahway, New Jersey. She was one of eleven children. Her father was a plumber, and when he died he left just about enough to pay his debts and bury him."

Williams rose slowly to his feet, still gripping the back of the chair, "I don't believe that you have the right to cross-question me about my private business, Inspector. Am I charged with being in the rackets?"

"Not yet. Sit down."

Williams dropped back unto the chair. Beads of perspiration glittered on his forehead.

"Let's be sensible about this, Earl. Somebody gave you the money to buy this place. I suggest that your benefactor was one Guy Severied. I suggest that he wasn't actuated by a philanthropic whim. I suggest you were paid to be silent about facts you had unearthed in the Pelham case."

Williams groaned under his breath.

"If there was a crime, Earl — if Dorothy Pelham was murdered — then by keeping silent you have become an accessory after the fact. You could go to the chair for it."

"There was no crime!" Williams cried. "I swear it!"

Bradley waited, his gaze unwavering.

"I swear to that, Bradley. If you examined my record, you'll know there wasn't a single black mark against me. You'll know that I had a high rating, that my honesty was never questioned. I never covered a crime in my life. I never took a bribe."

"This farm was just a present … given to you in gratitude for having failed to find out anything about Dorothy Pelham? It won't wash, Earl."

"But it's true!"

"Ah, then you admit the way you handled the Pelham case resulted in your receiving a large gift of cash!"

"But I tell you there was no evidence! Ask Bonesteel, the private dick who took over after we gave up the case."

"I have. He agrees with you. But he came on the case after you, Earl. It's possible you had destroyed any evidence there was by that time."

"No, no, *no!*" Williams raised his hands, held them hard against his temples.

Bradley sighed. "Let's have it, Earl. You know what happened to Mrs. Pelham. You've been paid to keep quiet about it. Come clean … and perhaps there may be a chance for you to stay here on your farm."

"A … a chance to … to stay here?"

"God damn it, man, this is no game! If you refuse to help me you're coming back to town tonight, charged with conspiracy and possibly murder!"

Williams pressed his forehead against the back of the chair. "Oh, God," he murmured. "Oh, God!"

"Well, Earl?"

Williams looked up, his eyes stricken. "There … there's nothing I can tell you, Bradley. Except this. There was no crime in connection with Dorothy Pelham's death."

"Then she *is* dead?"

"Yes."

"Was it an accident?"

"Yes,"

"Then why … "

"Bradley, I have concealed facts, but I have concealed them with an absolutely clear conscience. I'd do it again. It wasn't the money. I would have kept shut if there hadn't been a dime involved."

"All right, Earl, I'll accept that." Bradley leaned forward. "But two people have been murdered in the last forty-eight hours because they also knew that secret. You and Severied may be next. You haven't the right to keep that secret any longer! Is that clear?"

"I have to," said Williams wearily. "Bradley, this farm is my life now. My daughter has gone through college and is making a success in business, My wife had an operation a year ago. These things have been made possible because of the gratitude of a friend. I'm not letting him down now, Bradley. I'm not letting him down, whatever you choose to — "

"You're a sucker Earl! If you don't talk, you'll endanger the life of your friend. That's not gratitude … it's stupidity!"

"I'm sorry."

Bradley stood up. "So am I. Get your hat and coat. You're coming back to New York with me."

"All right," said Williams. "If that's the way it has to be." He started to rise from his chair.

"Forget it, Earl," said a voice from behind him.

Guy Severied walked out of the dark corridor and into the warmth of the kitchen. He looked tired and disheveled. His eyes were puffy and red-rimmed. His hands, as he extracted a cigarette from a silver case, weren't steady.

Bradley gave him a fleeting smile. He was obviously not surprised. "Mercy," he said, "I thought I'd have to start working Earl over before you'd come out of that hallway."

"You knew I was there?" Guy asked.

"You shouldn't leave Racquet Club Specials burning in country kitchens."

"It doesn't matter," said Guy. "There's no reason Earl should take the rap for this."

"He can't help himself," said Bradley. "It's a serious rap. When a policeman conspires to conceal a crime …"

"He's told you over and over that there was no crime!" Guy said.

"What *did* happen?"

Guy shook his head. "No, dice, Inspector."

"I don't want to arrest you, Severied," Bradley said.

"I can imagine!" Guy said. He gave Bradley a wry smile. "Policemen just hate to make arrests."

"The reason is I can't charge you with murder, so presently you'd both be out on bail. The murderer will then know where you are. That clear?"

"Quite!" Guy's face was hard. "So why arrest us? It isn't

going to do any good, you know. We're not going to talk. Not yet."

"When?" said Bradley sharply.

"Inspector, you're pretty shrewd," Guy said, "I didn't believe you'd come so close to the answers. Especially in such a short time. It's that cleverness, Mr. Bradley, that makes me determined not to talk. Maybe you'll solve the case without us. Until I'm sure you can't … " Guy shrugged.

"Do you know who murdered Gloria and her father, Severied?"

"No," Guy said.

"If it were Pelham, would you try to shield him?"

"No," said Guy without hesitation, "You know what was in the letter Gloria wrote and left with Linda?"

"I know what Gloria said she wrote."

"From reading that letter would the murderer know about Earl Williams?"

Guy whistled, "Nice point, Inspector. Neat. I'd missed it. Of course he knows … "

"Then I'm arresting you," said Bradley. "Because you're not safe here either. Get your things."

"But, Bradley," Williams protested.

"Sorry, I want you both alive."

***

Afterward Bradley blamed himself. If he hadn't been so concerned with thinking of some means of persuading Guy to talk, he would have paid more attention. The dog, Squire, really tried to warn him.

While Guy and Williams were getting into their things.

Squire stalked over to the door, hackles raised, and began sniffing, and growling at the crack. But Bradley didn't notice … at least not consciously.

"Do we go in irons?" Guy asked, as he came back from the hall.

"I don't own any," said Bradley. "Damn it, man, why don't you talk? Can't you see, once I know, there'll be no use in more killings?"

"Sorry, Inspector." Guy was sardonic. "I've been at some pains and expense and personal misery to keep this secret for five years. I'm not giving yet. Not yet. Not till I know it's the only way."

Williams joined them and they went out onto the back porch, locking the whining Squire inside. They walked down the path, Williams lighting the way with a flash. Then it happened.

There were several sharp reports … tongues of flame stabbed the darkness. The torch dropped from Williams' hand and buried itself in the snow. Guy cried out.

Bradley made a dive for the torch and recovered it. For an instant he saw Guy down on his knees, clutching at his left side. Then he ran. Before he reached the corner of the house. he heard a motor spring to life … the whir of chains as a car started quickly.

A red taillight was careening down the drive as Bradley sprang into his own car. He stepped on the starter button. Nothing happened. He got out, lifted the engine hood.

"The son of a bitch!" he said.

The torch revealed a mess of twisted wires, ripped from their moorings.

19

WILLIAMS was whimpering as he tried to haul Guy toward the porch.

"For God's sake, Earl, get hold of yourself," Bradley said, Then the flash picked up Williams and the unconscious Guy, and Bradley saw why Williams had dropped the light in the first place. He held his right hand close to his stomach, smashed and bleeding.

Inside the house Squire was trying to tear the door down. Bradley took Guy under the arms and pulled him up on the porch. Williams fumbled with his key, left-handed, and got the door open. As they dragged Guy into the kitchen, a woman, in a quilted dressing gown and with paper curlers in her hair, joined them,

"My wife," Williams said.

"Telephone the nearest doctor," Bradley ordered.

Mrs. Williams proved far more efficient in the crisis than her husband. The doctor was phoned; blankets were brought to cover Guy. Bradley did not want to move him farther until the doctor came. The murderer's bullet had struck him in the left side.

Bradley undid his vest and shirt, and swore softly. "You're all so God damned noble!" he said, Then he remembered his car, "Get a garage-man out here. Have him bring a car I can hire in case he can't get mine rolling."

Williams phoned. Sweat was running down his face. His hand was hurting him cruelly. He came back to Bradley, who was staring down at Guy's white face,

"They were waiting for you, Bradley," he said,

"For *me!*" Bradley was explosive. "Not me, Williams. For you and Severied! You've got to talk, Earl. There's no end in this if you don't."

"I can't, Bradley. Not till Mr. Severied says okay."

"If he dies, by Jesus, you'll have him on your conscience."

"I'll have to risk that."

Bradley paced up and down the room, chewing on the stem of his empty pipe. Mrs. Williams reappeared, silently, with a basin of warm water and bandages. She went to work on her husband's hand. Bradley could hear the hiss of Williams' breath as she touched the raw wound.

"There's something you *can* tell me, Earl," Bradley said, stopping in front of Williams. "What's the regular routine in the Missing Persons Bureau? Take the Pelham case. You investigated her home, her friends, her husband. No clues. She had walked out into the blue and vanished. Then what?"

"We checked on Pelham … where he'd been. There was the possibility of homicide, but we couldn't get any evidence."

"But there must be other routine checkups."

"Oh, those. We check on any accidents that may have happened. We follow up motor smashes … injuries in the subway or on buses or ferries. If it's summer, we check the beaches for drownings. If there've been any explosions or public disasters of any kind, we follow up the injured."

"About Dorothy Pelham?" said Bradley grimly.

Williams shook his head. "We were never able to connect her with … with anything." He looked away.

Bradley stared at him, impotent fury in his eyes. "So you're still being a little gentleman! What the hell, Earl? The woman's dead! Nothing can hurt her now."

"Bradley, for the love of heaven, see how I'm fixed. It's up to him." Williams jerked a thumb at Guy. "It's got to be up to him."

"What did Jerry Bonesteel mean when he said Dorothy Pelham was fond of the boys?"

"I … I don't know."

"Was she some kind of a nymph?"

"I never came across anything of that sort," Williams said. "I don't know what Jerry was talking about."

Mrs. Williams stood up. She had finished wrapping a crude bandage around her husband's hand. "Mr. Bradley, Earl has always been a square shooter," she said. "If he thinks his loyalty lies with his friend, nothing in the world will make him betray it."

"All right!" said Bradley. "All *right!*"

The doctor and the garage man arrived simultaneously. The mechanic reported no real damage to Bradley's car. The connections had been pulled loose, but there was nothing broken. He'd have it running in ten minutes.

The doctor and Bradley carried Guy to a front bedroom. The doctor examined the wound. Finally he said, "I think he'll make it, Inspector. It's nasty. Bullet tore quite a hole. Hit a rib, though. I don't think anything vital has been injured."

"Hospital case?"

"Good God, yes. Infection is the greatest danger."

Bradley went back into the kitchen and pulled on his overcoat. Williams followed him, looking miserable.

"I wish I could help, Inspector. I know how it is how you

feel. I've been held out on in my time. But I feel better than I did when you first came."

"So?"

"I was afraid it was … was … "

"Severied?"

Williams nodded. "It put me in a hell of a spot. In a way, getting shot has … has taken a load off my mind."

"Glad you've got something to console you," snapped Bradley. "I haven't."

"If there's anything else I can do … "

"Else?" Bradley laughed. "Maybe you've served your purpose, Earl. Acting as a target. Desperate fellow, our murderer."

"You think he'll come back here?"

"No. I don't. He must have guessed, when he saw me taking you both back, that you hadn't spilled. But he knows I'm breathing right down his neck. I think my name's up next."

"You've got ideas, Bradley?"

"I'm lousy with 'em," Bradley said.

***

"You're still up," Bradley said.

Celia Devon opened the door wider to admit him. "I didn't know there were any curfew laws, Mr. Bradley."

"It's four in the morning," Bradley said.

"I'm past the age when I concern myself with beauty sleep."

"Where's Miss Prayne?"

"Asleep, thank the Lord. I packed her off with a heavy sedative early in the evening. She was all in."

There was no friendliness in Bradley's tone. "Where have you been yourself all evening?"

"Here, Inspector. Aren't you being just a little grim?"

"We nearly had two more corpses on our hands tonight." said Bradley. "We are not amused."

"Inspector!"

"So Miss Prayne has been dead to the world since early this evening?"

"Since about nine o'clock."

"Where's your car? It's not downstairs in the school where it belongs."

Miss Devon's lower lip caught between her teeth for a moment. Then she said, "You'd better come in and sit down. I'll fix you something hot to drink."

"Thanks. My social life has been checked for the moment. The car. Where is it?"

"Johnny has it," Miss Devon said.

"Since when?"

"He took it about six o'clock this evening."

"What for?"

"He … he went to Delaware, Inspector."

"Delaware?"

"Those kids are still whistling in the dark, Mr. Bradley. They think they may find a suspect for you outside our little lot. Johnny's getting a list of the people who were at the shooting lodge last week."

"He should have asked permission to leave town. Anyone go with him?"

"No. You didn't give orders … "

"Are Johnny and Pelham at all intimate?"

"Why … why, no, I mean, they always seemed to get along well enough. Johnny's much younger."

"It's the matter of Pelham's gun," said Bradley. "It was used again tonight. Somebody in a car. Miss Devon?"

Miss Devon evaded his eyes. "Everybody owns cars these days."

"Or you can hire them to drive yourself."

"Incidentally," said Miss Devon, "I am a licensed driver, and Barney Oldfield tips his hat to me when we pass."

"Mercy," said Bradley. For a moment his eyes softened. "Don't tell me you're in the red-herring business too, Miss Devon?"

Miss Devon frowned. "If the damn fool would get the idea of mass killings out of his head, I'd be half inclined to … to … "

"Give him a break."

She nodded.

"That's a hard-boiled attitude, Miss Devon."

"Blackmail ranks high on my slime list," said Miss Devon cooly. "Gloria and Douglas got what was coming to them."

"You haven't asked me who tonight's victims were," Bradley said.

"Haven't I? I took it for granted, I'm afraid. Of course, it was Guy. And you, too, perhaps?"

"Guy will live, if it interests you."

"It does."

"The other victim was a man named Williams. Shot in the hand."

"A dairy farmer?" asked Miss Devon calmly.

"Madam, I think I will come in and sit down after all," said Bradley.

There were still hot coals in the grate.

Bradley sat down on the couch, but he did not take off his coat.

"If you won't have something hot, how about brandy?" Miss Devon asked,

He watched her fill a glass and bring it to him. She sat down opposite him and automatically reached for the knitting bag that hung over the back of the chair.

"So you knew about our dairy farmer?" Bradley said.

"Oh, yes. Guy drove me out to the farm once. It seems he became interested in the man — Williams, isn't it? — while he was investigating Dorothy's disappearance." Miss Devon's eyes lowered to the knitting. "I think Guy helped him financially. He's really very generous."

"I remember. He kept Gloria equipped. Under pressure. Was Williams turning a screw, too?"

"I haven't the faintest idea."

"Perhaps you can tell me something about Dorothy. Did she run around a lot with other men?"

"Decidedly not."

Bradley frowned. "A very reliable source has told me that she was 'fond of the boys.'"

"Perhaps you had better check on your 'reliable source,' Mr. Bradley.' Not a sensitive person."

"I don't follow you. You have all told me the Pelhams were extremely happy together. Yet a trained observer …"

"The Pelhams *were* happy. But do people always love each other equally, Inspector? Is marriage always synonymous with a grand passion?'

"I suppose not. What are you trying to say?"

"I'm trying to say that your observer made a mistake. He mistook Dorothy's attitude toward one man as being symptomatic of her attitude toward all men. A conclusion jumper, Mr. Bradley."

Bradley's eyes narrowed. He drained the jigger of brandy and put it down. He stood up.

"Thank you again," he said. He stared over her head at the wall, fumbling for his pipe and the red tobacco tin. "When do you expect Johnny back?"

"Sometime early in the morning. He thought he could make the trip in twelve or fourteen hours. Why?"

"I want to see him, In fact, I want to see you all — you and

Pat and that voting man — at my office at nine o'clock."

"Another grilling, inspector?"

"No," said Bradley. He looked down at her. "If I get there myself, I'm going to arrest the murderer."

Miss Devon lowered the knitting to her lap. "You think he will ..."

"I think he will not like the idea," said Bradley.

20

GEORGE PELHAM parked his car outside the building where he lived. He got out, locked the car door, and walked across the pavement toward the building entrance. His walk was unsteady, as if he were drunk. His overcoat was wet; his brown hat was sodden. He leaned against the door, lacking the strength to push it open with his hands.

The foyer was dark, except for the reflection of a light over the switchboard at the far end near the elevators. Pelham started forward, heels clicking noisily on the tile floor.

In a dark alcove which opened into a doctor's office, a figure stirred. Pelham didn't notice it. A hand reached out and caught his sleeve.

"George!"

Pelham stopped dead in his tracks. The nerve at the corner of his mouth twitched violently.

"Linda!" he said in a hoarse voice. "You … you startled me."

She came out of the darkness, "Oh, George, where have you been, sweet? I've been frantic about you … hunting for you for hours. Calling all the places I could think of."

"I was just … just looking," he said.

"George you're shaking!"

"Bushed," he said.

"I'll come up with you and fix you some coffee while you get out of those wet things."

"I … That would be swell," he said. "I guess I could go for something."

The elevator man was studiously uninterested as he ferried them up to Pelham's floor. Pelham tried to get his key in the lock, but his fingers were so unsteady that Linda had to take the key from him. His face looked gray when she switched on the light inside the door.

"Cold," he said. "It's cold as hell."

"Where have you been, George?"

"Around … hunting for Guy. Long Island … the Yacht Club … night spots. No one has seen him."

"Your feet are soaked, darling. And you're wet to the skin, Get into pajamas and a warm bathrobe. I'll rustle something in the kitchen."

"Coffee would be best," he said wearily.

Ten minutes later they were sitting on the couch to percolator chugging on the table in front of them.

"I've sent to the drugstore f or some bromides for you, George. You've got to get some sleep."

"Sleep!" he said, "Cripes!'"

"You shouldn't have gone off by yourself, George."

"Why not?"

"Bradley's watching us all. He'll want you to explain."

"Then I'll explain! I have a right to hunt up Guy. He's my friend. Damn it, Linda, what's Guy up to? Why is he hiding?"

"Guy knows what he's doing."

"Sure he does. But what is he doing? Linda, is there something about this I don't know? Guy's concealing something. Are you in on it too?"

"George!"

"Something's going on behind my back. Bradley didn't pick Dorothy out of thin air. I've been trying to tell myself he's a fool; but, God damn it, he isn't! He had a reason. Somebody told him something. I've got to know what it is! I've got to!"

"Darling, please!"

"If there's something about Dorothy I haven't been told …" He covered his face with his hands. "I can't go on without knowing, Linda. I can't!"

The doorbell rang. Linda went to answer it. "That'll be the boy from the drugstore," she said.

It was Bradley. Behind him, glowering, was Rube Snyder.

Bradley looked past Linda to Pelham, huddled on the couch.

"Captain, I'd like to borrow your car keys."

At the sound of Bradley's voice Pelham jumped to his feet. "What are you doing here?"

"Your car keys!" said Bradley.

"They're in my bedroom … on the bureau. I … "

"I'll get them," Linda said.

"What do you want with the keys?" Pelham asked.

"I want to look for a gun."

"Oh, for God's sake!"

"Severied was shot tonight ... with your gun, Pelham."

"Guy *shot!*"

"You wouldn't know anything about it, I suppose," said Bradley grimly.

"When did it happen? Where?"

Linda came out of the bedroom with the keys.

"Guy's dead!" Pelham said.

"*What!* George, I don't believe it! Inspector Bradle y — "

"He's not dead," said Bradley. "The murderer missed killing him. Blew quite a hole in him though."

Pelham swayed on his feet. "I've got to go to him. He'll need someone. Where is he, inspector?"

"I'm afraid you're going to have to stay here for a while, Captain. I want to know where you've been this evening."

"George and I have been here together for quite some time," Linda said quickly.

"I know. All of twenty minutes. The keys, please." He took them and passed them to Rube. "Search," he said. "Don't get intrigued with some radio program."

"Aw, Red, cut it out." Rube pocketed the keys and disappeared.

"Well, Captain?"

"I've been hunting for Guy since about six o'clock," Pelham said, sinking back on the couch.

"And you, Miss Marsh?"

"I've been at the shop most of the evening," Linda said. "But I was worried about George. He was in a state. I kept calling here and getting no answer. Finally I came here and waited for him."

"How long ago?"

"About an hour."

"Was anyone with you at the shop before that?"

"No." Linda's voice was angry. "You had pretty successfully disrupted my day, Inspector. I had to catch up with the work on my desk."

Bradley turned to Pelham. "I suppose you saw people in the course of the evening who could check your alibi?"

"I suppose so," Pelham said.

"Who?"

"God, I don't know who I saw! There must have been plenty of people. I … "

Bradley interrupted. "Do you remember a man named Williams who handled your wife's case? The murderer took a shot at him tonight, too."

Pelham wavered to his feet again. "Why?" he cried. *"Why?"*

"I thought perhaps you could tell me."

For the second time in twenty-four hours Pelham went off his head. He took the front of Bradley's coat in his hands and shook him. "You can't do this to me! You've been worrying at me from the start … prodding, poking, yanking at me! *I'm* the one to be asking questions! You know what happened to Dorothy. Tell me, or by God I'll—"

"Sit down!" Bradley said. He said it so quietly that it checked Pelham in full flight. "I'll tell you what happened to your wife," said Bradley deliberately, "tomorrow morning at nine o'clock. I want you at my office then. You too, Miss Marsh."

Linda's voice was very low. "Then you … you know something, Mr. Bradley? Guy told you something?"

"He wouldn't, and now he can't," said Bradley. "No, Miss Marsh, I don't know the answer yet, But I will at nine tomorrow."

"But how — "

"The murderer is going to tell me," said Bradley. He looked at Pelham, who had sunk down on the couch, the image of despair. He seemed not to be hearing the conversation. Linda drew Bradley aside.

"Does he … does he have to know, Inspector, if it is something that would hurt him?"

"It will supply the motive," said Bradley.

"But if you *know*, does it have to be *used?"*

"The murderer will be tried before a jury, Miss Marsh. You don't get convictions without supplying them with a motive."

"Then you can't make it easy for — "

"I'm sorry, Miss Marsh. After going back to the Praynes' to wait for young Curtin. There's just a chance he may have stumbled onto something. I advise you to go home and get some rest. Tomorrow is going to be a tough day."

21

RUBE SNYDER was waiting for Bradley on the sidewalk.

"No gun," he reported.

"Give the keys to the elevator man and we'll get moving," Bradley said.

Rube gave Bradley a sidelong glance when he rejoined him, and they started downtown, He had seen that tight, pinched look on the inspector's face before and he knew what it meant. They were coming to the end of a case, and victory or defeat was hanging in the balance. Something had to work … something Bradley had planned.

"You phoned Julius?" Bradley asked.

"Sure, Red. He'll be at the Praynes' about five. That's what I *think* he said. He was so damn sore at bein' woke up I couldn't hardly make out what he was sayin'. But I'm pretty sure it was 'yes.'"

Bradley smiled faintly. "He'll come. He can't help himself."

"Say, look here, Red … what are you up to? You can't put nothin' over on me. You're foolin' around with loaded dice. You're worried."

"Huh!" grunted Bradley. He drove several blocks in silence. "Wouldn't you think, Rube, after all these years I'd stop feeling sorry for people?"

"Yeah, I would. Don't tell me you're sorry for the guy who's knocked off two people and tried to get two others."

"Yes. In a way I am, Rube. But I'm sorrier for someone else."

"You know," said Rube, "it would be better if you didn't say nothin' unless you're gonna tell me the works. You know who done this?"

"Beyond a shadow of a doubt. Rube. But I haven't got evidence. That's where the gamble comes in. I hope to get it before morning."

"Where we goin' now?"

"To look at old newspaper files," said Bradley.

***

He went through the files at headquarters while Rube stood by.

"If you'd tell me what you're lookin' for, Red, I could help."

"I don't know what I'm looking for," Bradley said.

In the end he apparently found something he wanted. He cut a handful of clippings from one of the newspapers, put them in his inside pocket, and got wearily to his feet.

"That's that," he said. "Now for Julius."

"What about me?" Rube asked.

"I don't care what you do, Rube. Better get some sleep."

"Look, Red, if you're pullin' somethin' screwy … "

Forget it," Bradley said.

***

Bradley took a taxi uptown to the Praynes'. There was a tiny night light burning over the door which led into the school, left for Johnny in case he returned with the car before morning.

Bradley went into the riding ring. A few feet from the door the place was cavernous and dark as a deserted cathedral. He walked over to the stand where he had sat the day before watching Pelham ride, and appropriated one of the wicker chairs. Automatically he stuffed the bowl of his pipe and struck a match to light it. As the flame illuminated his face, a crotchety voice spoke behind him.

"You *might* have asked me to meet you at the bottom of a well," said Mr. Julius. "You might have, but you chose this instead."

The old man, wrapped from eyes to ankles in his long black coat, came across the platform to where Bradley sat.

"What kind of hocus-pocus is this?" he demanded. "Get a man up at four-thirty in the morning! Keep him waiting in this mausoleum! Your idea of a joke, Bradley? Because, if it is, it's not funny. Not a damn bit funny."

"Mercy," said Bradley, "you've worked up a fine head of steam."

"So would you." The old man peered through the gloom at Bradley. "You're tired!" It was an accusation the way he said it.

"I've been moving around."

"And getting nowhere, I wager."

"Maybe not," said Bradley. "Did you bring the notes on those alibis with you?"

"Naturally … That's what you dragged me out of bed for, wasn't it? But I've not checked 'em yet. It'll take days."

"I don't care whether they check or not," said Bradley. "I'm mainly interested in the critical hours. Gloria left Johnny Curtin at El Morocco on Wednesday night. She wasn't seen after that. I think she was murdered between then and morning. Otherwise we'd have some clue as to where she eventually spent the night. I want to know where our friends say they were between midnight Wednesday and breakfast Thursday."

"That's simple," said Mr. Julius, *"if* they were telling the truth," He took his notes from his pocket and shuffled them into order. "Can't read in this light. But my mind still works."

"Pat: At Horse Show till about one o'clock. Drove home in murder car. Parked in the Crop and Spur. Went to bed."

Bradley nodded. His eyes were half closed, watching the smoke drift up from his pipe.

"Celia," the old man continued. "Spent evening at home. Says Prayne was there. He went to bed early. She sat up for Pat. Fixed some hot chocolate or some such slops for her when she came in. Went to bed.

"Curtin: At Horse Show early in evening. Picked Gloria up around eleven and look her to El Morocco. Quarreled. She left him after midnight. He went other places, hoping to find her and square things. No luck, he *says*. Went back to his hotel on the East Side. This one is full of holes, Bradley."

"So I see. Go on."

"Linda: At her shop late. Can't say exactly what time she left. Didn't pay attention to time. When she'd finished, went home to bed. There was no one at shop. Elevator man at her apartment may be able to tell what time she got home.

"Pelham: At Horse Show all evening. Left same time Pat did, but walked home. Said needed fresh air. Pat usually drove him. Not that night. Stopped for a drink. Doesn't remember where … just some bar on the way home.

"And that's that," concluded Mr. Julius. "Nothing on Severied, naturally, because I couldn't find him to question. Only Celia's word on Douglas Prayne … but then you don't suspect him now, unless you think it's a gang killing."

"Interesting suggestion," Bradley said.

"Make anything out of it?"

"Since an attempt was made on Severied's life tonight, I'll include him out."

"What's that!"

"The murderer took a shot at Severied early tonight. Nearly got him too."

"Great Scott! Look here, Bradley, have you ideas about this?"

Bradley nodded.

"Well? Well? *Well?"*

Bradley puffed at his pipe for a moment. "You know how this school is run?"

"No. I don't. And what the devil has that got to do with this?"

"Nothing," said Bradley. "Except I talked with Shea, the groom, and something he said caught my fancy. When you've ridden the twenty-fourth horse, you know all the answers."

"What kind of rubbish are you talking?"

"You start with horse number one and keep progressing till you get through with horse number twenty-four. Then you get your diploma. Well, I've ridden the twenty-four horses in this case, and I know the answers — all of 'em."

"What are the answers?"

"If I told you about the twenty-four horses, you'd know yourself."

Mr. Julius banged his ear trumpet on the arm of his chair.

"All right, *all right!* If you want to play games, go ahead; tell me."

"Twenty-four clues," said Bradley. "Hang onto your hat.

"One: Guy Severied and George Pelham have been close friends for years.

"Two: Guy Severied did not love Gloria Prayne … but they were engaged to he married.

"Three: Linda Marsh is thirty-four years old."

"What the hell kind of a clue is that?" Mr. Julius exploded.

"Hush," said Bradley, grinning.

"*Four:* Gloria had an extensive and expensive wardrobe, purchased by Severied.

"*Five:* Gloria was afraid she was going to be murdered and wrote a letter which would expose the murderer.

"*Six:* Severied knew about it.

"*Seven:* Gloria's body was kept hidden for two days.

"*Eight:* The keys to the Prayne car were kept on a table in the tack room, and everyone connected with the case knew it.

"*Nine:* The murderer had a key to Guy Severied's apartment.

"*Ten:* Douglas Prayne hot-footed it to see Severied, talked with the murderer, and was shot.

"*Eleven:* Severied went into hiding.

"*Twelve:* George Pelham owns a gun of the type used in the second murder.

"*Thirteen:* Severied went to Pelham's apartment to find that gun and had to knock out Rube to get away.

"*Fourteen:* When Dorothy Pelham disappeared the only thing missing was her toothbrush.

"*Fifteen:* Johnny Curtin gave Gloria the air, and she went away mad.

"*Sixteen:* Guy Severied got stinking drunk before he heard of the murder.

"*Seventeen:* George Pelham is what our romantic lady novelists call 'a one-woman man.'

"*Eighteen:* Earl Williams owns a dairy farm in Peekskill, New York.

"*Nineteen:* Guy Severied never looks at expense accounts.

"*Twenty:* All women think that chains keep them from skidding on icy roads."

"For Pete's sake!" said Mr. Julius disgustedly.

"Twenty-one:" said Bradley, unmoved. "The Hotel Gansvoort burned to the ground in 1935."

"Bradley, stop it! You're off your trolley."

"Twenty-two: All unmarried women have a strong maternal complex."

"God save us!" said Mr. Julius.

"Twenty-three: The murderer had to have (a) access to Gloria's stationery; (b) access to Linda's desk; (c) access to Pelham's apartment to get his gun; (d) access to Severied's apartment; (e) access to an automobile.

"Twenty-four: The murderer had to be somebody Gloria Prayne trusted. She would never have allowed herself to be trapped by anyone she feared. Not Severied! He was the person she was mortally afraid of." Bradley drew a long breath. "Well, have you got it?"

"I have got," said Mr. Julius, "a headache. I think it ought to be grounds for dismissal for any policeman to read modern detective stories. Who the hell do you think you are ... Philo Vance, Ellery Queen? All this hooey!" The old man got up. "I never thought the day would come when you'd turn into a gibbering idiot, Go fancy on me, will you? Well, I won't even guess! I don't want to know?"

"Just the same, I'm grateful to you for your help ... and for listening," said Bradley.

"Humph!" said Mr. Julius. "I'm going back to my bed. Consider yourself lucky if I ever give you five minutes of my time again. Good night."

He stomped down off the platform, across the tanbark, and out the door onto the street.

Bradley watched him go, smiling. Then the look of amusement faded slowly from his face. He tamped down the tobacco in the bowl of his pipe and lit another match. Just as he drew in on the flame, a voice spoke behind him—a woman's voice, cold and implacable.

"Don't turn around, Mr. Bradley, and don't dare to move. I have this gun leveled straight at the back of your head."

The flame burned slowly down the stick of the match until it reached Bradley's fingers.

He dropped it, and the place was almost completely dark again.

"How did you like my summation of the case, Miss Marsh?" he asked quietly.

"I thought it fatally good," said Linda Marsh.

Bradley sat perfectly still, "I didn't think you'd risk it," he said. "But I had hopes."

"Hopes?"

"I told you I was going to be here." Bradley's voice was mild.

"Just what did you expect me to do?" Linda said. She sounded metallic, hard, grimly purposeful. "Wait until morning for you to arrest me with dramatic effect at headquarters?"

"I thought perhaps you would do some thinking," Bradley said. "I thought perhaps you would realize the futility of going on with this and surrender peacefully."

"Celia called you an optimist the other night," Linda said. "She was right. Why should I surrender? I can still get away with this, Inspector. I can still live my life."

Bradley was as motionless as if he'd been carved out of stone. "Julius has the evidence," he reminded her.

Linda laughed. It was a harsh, grating sound. "You had him thoroughly confused. You spun your web so subtly that the poor old fool is more at sea than ever."

"Do you think," Bradley asked, "that Pelham will marry you in the end?"

"I think he will," Linda said. "But not if he got to know. It would blow what's left of his world to pieces. That, Mr. Bradley, is why you have come to the end of the trail. I'm sorry for you. You've been doing your job."

"And I'm sorry for you," Bradley said.

"Damn you for that!"

"If you hadn't had to pile it up … If it hadn't been I or Douglas Prayne …"

"There's no use our discussing it, Mr. Bradley. You know the answers, as you told Julius. One of us has to die for the other to go on living."

"It would be easier to talk if you'd come around where I could see you," Bradley said. "But I suppose it will be simpler from behind. You took care of the others that way."

For the first time Linda's voice broke. "For God's sake, Mr. Bradley, isn't there some way out of this? I'm fighting for my life, for George's. You know that. I thought with Gloria gone that would be the end of it. I thought it made me safe … made George safe. I thought Guy would benefit. Then I found she'd told her father. I couldn't stop then. I had to go on."

Bradley started to tap out his pipe in the palm of his hand.

"Don't move!" Linda warned. "I'm not taking chances."

Bradley sat still. "I know what you were up against," he said.

"I thought I'd be safe, even after that," Linda said. "But you came into it and stumbled across the line that led you to the truth. My only chance was to keep Guy and Williams from talking."

"It's like a snowball," Bradley said. "Murder always is. Now you are going to kill me. When Guy recovers, he's going to realize why. You'll have to go on. You'll have to finish the job you tried tonight. Guy … then Williams. Do you know what will happen then?"

Linda's voice sounded parched. "What?"

"Celia Devon is no fool. She suspects George. Wrong, of course. But she's guessed the secret, or will, Sooner or later she'll know it was you. You'll have to keep on. Perhaps in the end George himself will have to die … although you've done all this for him. You're out over your head, Miss Marsh. You can't win. But I'll give you a chance to save something."

"You're not in a position to offer terms, Mr. Bradley."

"If you'll submit to arrest," said Bradley, "I promise you that Pelham need never know the truth about Dorothy. You've done all this to keep him from knowing. I offer you the chance to win on that score. If you refuse, in the long run the thing will catch up with you and there will be no secrets kept from anyone."

There was silence for a moment. He could hear her deep, labored breathing.

Then she said, "I'll take a chance on winning, Mr. Bradley. I'm sorry. But I *have* to take it."

At that precise moment there was a sound of smashing glass and the tiny light of the door was gone, the place plunged into complete darkness. There was a blast of flame from behind Bradley, but in that split second he had pitched sideways out of his chair and roiled off the edge of the platform to the tanbark. Linda's gun exploded again, echoing and re-echoing.

Then Bradley said quietly, "You can't make it, Miss Marsh. There are men in every exit. Your statement has been taken down by a police stenographer. I'm sorry. I would have kept my word if you'd accepted terms. Drop your gun on the platform."

He could hear her strangled gasp for breath. He kept his head below the level of the platform lest she should fire again in the direction of his voice. Her gun did spout flame. There was a heavy thud.

"Lights!" Bradley shouted.

Instantly the overhead lights came on. Bradley was on his feet. Plain-clothes men converged on the platform. Linda Marsh lay, face down, just behind Bradley's overturned chair. She had, after all, made her own decision.

Bradley turned away. He looked gray and tired. “Thanks, Corcoran,” he said. “I had to use you instead of Rube. I was afraid he wouldn’t hold his fire long enough. You got her statement?”

“Every word of it, Inspector. You’ve solved your case.”

Bradley sighed. “There may still be a thing or two to do about it.”

***

Bradley was late in reaching his office the next morning. He had been through a session with the commissioner.

When he walked into the room he discovered Pat, Johnny, Miss Devon, and Pelham waiting for him. The lines in his face seemed to grow deeper.

He walked around behind his desk, stood there for a minute looking through some reports, and then with a kind of reluctance faced his visitors.

“I thought after you’d seen the papers this morning you’d realize that it wasn’t necessary for you to come here,” he said.

“We simply can’t believe this,” Johnny said, He held up a copy of a newspaper, headlines black under a picture of Linda Marsh.

LOVE KILLER AND SUICIDE
Famous Fashion Designer Murders Rival

“I’m sorry, but it’s true enough,” Bradley said. He lowered his eyes and began talking rapidly. “I owe you an apology, Captain Pelham. I was certain these killings were connected with your wife’s disappearance. I was wrong.” He glanced up, saw Miss Devon’s shrewd eyes fixed on him, and looked away again. “Linda was thirty-four years old, and there had been just one love in her life all these years — Severied. Gloria had some sort of hold on Severied and was forcing him into a marriage.

When he threatened to rebel against her blackmailing she became frightened and wrote a letter exposing him as her potential murderer in case he should go to such lengths. She gave the letter to Linda to keep, being unaware of Linda's feeling for Severied. Linda opened the letter and discovered why Severied had turned away from her. She destroyed the letter, waited for an opportunity to prepare a duplicate, and then her decks were clear."

"Why the duplicate?" asked Miss Devon in a steady voice. "Why not simply destroy it?"

"She couldn't be certain that Gloria hadn't mentioned the existence of the letter to someone else," Bradley explained. "She took no chances on that. She instantly produced the letter, thus throwing suspicion away from herself."

"But, damn it, I simply can't understand it!" Pelham said. "When Linda was with me she seemed to ..."

"There is no doubt Miss Marsh was extremely fond of you, Captain," said Bradley, "but she was in love with Severied. Once she had killed Gloria she found herself caught in a web from which she couldn't escape. She was forced to kill Douglas Prayne when he guessed that she was the murderer. In the end she actually had to make an attempt on Severied, who had also hit on the truth about her."

"Where was Gloria killed?" Miss Devon asked.

"At the dress shop. She went there after leaving Johnny at El Morocco. Linda was working late at the shop, as she often did. She strangled Gloria, kept the body hidden there for two days in an unused storeroom to which only she had access. On Saturday night, while everyone was excited about the Horse Show, she took the car keys from the tack room and drove to her shop. There is an alley for trucks at the rear. She dragged Gloria's body out onto a loading platform and rolled it into the rumble seat. The rest you know."

Pelham stared dully at Bradley. "And you learned nothing

about Dorothy? There's no new evidence?"

"Nothing. Not a shred," said Bradley, his eyes on the paper-littered desk.

Pelham got up from his chair, turned, and went quickly out of the room. Bradley came around the desk to where Johnny and Pat were sitting together.

"This has been tough on you two," he said, "But there's no reason why it should spoil your lives." He smiled wryly. "But try to be a little less complicated than your friends and relatives have been."

"You can count on that," Johnny said. "I'm marrying Pat today … now, if she'll have me. I'm taking her up to my farm in Millbrook, and that will be that."

Bradley watched them leave, and then he gave Miss Devon, who remained stolidly in her chair, a questioning look.

"I have the highest regard for your abilities as a detective, Mr. Bradley," she said, "but you are a terrible liar."

"Mercy, was it as bad as that?" he asked unhappily.

"I think you got away with it," said Miss Devon, "but you and I know that this story of yours is the sheerest twaddle. I'd like to know the real answer."

Bradley said, "Did you ever drink a scotch and soda at nine-thirty in the morning?"

"No, but there has to be a first time for everything."

"Come with me, then. I'm going off duty and there's a very good bar across the street."

***

"That story in the papers will hold water," said Bradley, looking up from his glass. He and Miss Devon were sitting in a booth in Bradley's bar. "Severied is quite willing to be the goat. I talked to him at the hospital before I gave it out."

"Guy would," said Miss Devon. "But why? Why not the

truth, whatever it is."

"Because," said Bradley gravely, "for five years Guy Severied has gone through hell to keep the truth hidden, and Linda Marsh committed two murders for the same cause."

"But see here … "

"It's a strange tale, Miss Devon. The story of the love of a man for his best friend, and of a woman for that same friend.

"Dorothy Pelham, as we suspected all along, was the key to the whole affair. Dorothy Pelham, who was 'crazy about the boys.' You doubted that, because under that acid veneer of yours you really think well of people. But Dorothy Pelham didn't deserve your confidence. I suspect that from the time she and Pelham were married she was never faithful to him.

"Guy Severied had reason to know this. Long before Pelham ever met Dorothy, she and Severied had had an affair. In fact, it was Severied who introduced her to Pelham. Then, while Severied was away on a big-game-hunting expedition, Pelham courted Dorothy and married her.

"Severied was delighted when he heard it. He was extremely fond of them both. He thought that with marriage Dorothy would settle down. But she didn't. She continued to play around. Severied tried to persuade her to give it up.

"He knew what it would mean to Pelham if he ever found out the truth.

"Dorothy wasn't having any. Instead, she tried to renew their old relationship. On the night that Dorothy disappeared she went to a hotel, took a suite there, and telephoned Severied to come and see her. He refused at first. Finally he agreed, but only because he decided that it was an opportunity to have it out with her once and for all." Bradley drew a deep breath. "The important point, Miss Devon, is that the hotel was the Gansvoort."

"Good Lord!" Miss Devon's tone was horrified.

"That night, as you know," Bradley continued, "the Gansvoort burned to the ground. Fifty or sixty people were burned to death. Dorothy Pelham was one of them. Severied was with her, but in the ensuing panic they were separated. He escaped. She did not." Bradley knocked the cold ashes from his pipe. "Severied was then confronted with a problem. If he told Pelham that Dorothy had died in the fire, he would have to explain how he knew it. He would have to confess that he had been there with her, alone. No one, not even Pelham, his best friend, would believe that he had gone there to break things off.

"Severied had to decide whether it was better for Pelham never to know what had happened to his wife and still retain his belief in her and his best friend or to know that she had never been faithful to him and live with the gnawing suspicion that Severied had double-crossed him. Guy decided that it was better for George never to know,"

"I think he was right," Miss Devon said.

"It was a costly decision. Once he had made it he could never go back on it without dealing George a body blow. Naturally, he went through the motions of helping George in his search for Dorothy. He even paid the private-detective fees. But before that he ran into his first trouble. Earl Williams, the policeman who handled the case for the department, following ordinary routine, finally stumbled on the truth. Guy admitted it and sold Williams on keeping quiet. No crime had been committed. Williams agreed.

"Nothing else cropped up for almost three years, and then things really got tough. Gloria was at Guy's apartment one day. He left her to do an errand, and she began looking at papers and letters on his desk. I gather she had no very strong sense of private property. In the process she found a secret drawer. In it was a written agreement between Severied and Williams, disclosing the whole story."

"Gloria had struck gold!" said Miss Devon.

"Quite so. She began a systematic blackmailing of Severied, which included marriage. Naturally Severied hated her guts. He must have made it so clear that she got frightened into writing the letter she left with Linda. If Guy pulled anything, he would pay. That was her notion.

"Now Linda Marsh had an ordinary amount of curiosity. Gloria had acted so queerly she couldn't resist opening the letter. And there the seed of murder was sown. Linda was in love with Pelham. It seemed likely that sooner or later George would marry her. But if this story, out of the past ever got to him, Pelham would crack into a thousand pieces. Linda was willing to go to any lengths to keep that knowledge from George.

"She planned carefully. It was simple enough to prepare a duplicate letter to substitute for the original and to borrow Pelham's automatic without his knowing it. Then she bided her time until the night Gloria left Johnny at El Morocco and went to Linda's shop. The actual details of the murder are exactly as I described them.

"Then her luck changed. She went to Guy's apartment to find the copy of that agreement, having taken a key from Gloria's purse. While she was there, Douglas Prayne arrived. Your brother-in-law, Miss Devon, was, I am afraid, not a nice person. Gloria had told him the facts. He saw himself in a position to continue the blackmail of Severied and lost no time in hurrying to Guy's apartment.

"He probably caught Linda red-handed going through Severied's desk, put two and two together, and accused her of murder. She shot him.

"Her next bad break came when I refused to believe in coincidences and began prying into Dorothy Pelham's past. She watched me drawing closer and closer to the truth. She thought if I put the heat on Guy and Williams they'd talk. She was on a sort of murder merry-go-round by then. There wasn't any stopping.

"Last night I gave her a chance. I offered to protect her secret if she would submit to arrest." Bradley shrugged.

"And now," said Miss Devon, "the secret ..."

"Will remain a secret," said Bradley. "Since there will be no trial, the motive I gave the press will stand up. George Pelham will never know the truth about his wife. Linda had courage, Miss Devon."

"One thing I don't understand," said Miss Devon, "What were you doing at the school last night and how did Linda happen to find you there?"

"I told her where I was going to be," said Bradley.

"You *what?*"

"I told her. I had a hunch she'd come after me."

"But the risk! The risk that she would shoot you down in cold blood."

"I had arranged a trap for her before I told her," Bradley said. "I had men stationed at the school. They let her go in and hide. She was covered every instant. I had to draw it fine."

"But why?"

Bradley gave her a small-boy smile. "Because I'm just a sucker, Miss Devon. I wanted to make a case against her if I could without dragging Pelham and the rest of you through the scandal of a trial. In a way, I wanted to do her a favor—to keep the secret she had struggled so hard to keep herself. Severied, too, deserves a break."

"But if she hadn't shot herself ..."

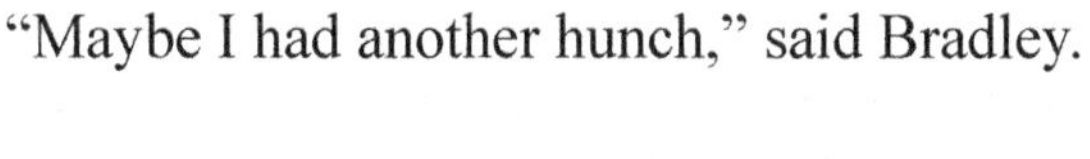

"Maybe I had another hunch," said Bradley.

About the author

Judson P. Philips, a Mystery Writers of America Grand Master Award winner, was born in Northfield, Mass. in 1903. He began his writing career in the pulp fiction magazines in 1924, while earning his journalism degree from Columbia University.

In 1939 he won the $10,000 Dodd Mead Mystery Contest, using the pen name Hugh Pentecost, for *Cancelled in Red*. This marked a turning point in his career, as he created a second body of work for slick magazines and paperbacks as Pentecost.

He used both names simultaneously, living in New York and later Connecticut, producing more than 500 works. One of his best-known series, The Park Avenue Hunt Club, appeared in *Detective Fiction Weekly*.

Philips owned a newspaper, and wrote columns for other newspapers. He owned an equity summer stock theater, "The Sharon Playhouse," where he wrote novels and produced plays. In the meantime, he wrote radio and film scripts for movies and television. He also hosted a political and arts program in Connecticut's "Northwest Corner," broadcast out of Torrington.

Philips was married five times and had four children. He died of complications from emphysema in 1989, at age 85, in Canaan, Connecticut.

A routine traffic stop ignites a bloody mob vendetta...

by GARY LOVISI

A "Vic Powers" action thriller with three extra exciting short stories!

BOLD VENTURE

The Original Adventures of Zorro by Johnston McCulley, Vol. 1
ZORRO

Made in the USA
Las Vegas, NV
13 January 2022

41306797R00111